THE LAST ROSE

NO MISTAKES

J.W. Irvan & Cheryl Bills

Gloucester & Midland Publishing

Books may be purchased by contacting the publisher at:
Gloucester & Midland Publishing, San Antonio, TX
https://gandmpub.wixsite.com/gloucesterandmidland
GloucesterAndMidland@gmail.com
or
https://theroseseries.wixsite.com/roses
theroseseries@gmail.com

Cover Design: Dani Leoni
Editor & Publisher: Gloucester & Midland Publishing
Library of Congress Catalog Number: 2017954690
ISBN: 978-0-9985490-1-9
1. Fiction; 2. Christian; 3. Spirituality; 4. Teens & Adults
First Edition
Printed in the USA by Amazon.com

Dedication

This book is dedicated to our parents, Vincent L. Irvan and Evelyn Irvan, with gratitude and love.

My dad was a very gifted writer and single-handedly inspired me to write my first short story. An avid reader, he left his vast library to me before he passed away along with his own short stories and poetry. Books he read while I played in the yard, I am now reading. A theologian, he had an unmatched vocabulary and it filtered down to all four of his kids. Suffice to say, if not for his influence you wouldn't be reading this book right now.

The same can be said for our mother, but for different reasons. She sets a Christ-like example (for her children as well as anyone who knows her) that is life-changing to say the least. I've never heard her curse because she never has. She has endured the weight of devastating life events and circumstances and if I went into detail, your mouth would drop wide open. But she has trusted the Lord through it all. Just a fraction of what she's gone though would break me. I've never seen such faith. She didn't have to tell us what Jesus meant to her (although she often did) because we could see it. She is the strongest human I have ever known. I think when she enters heaven, everything will stop and all eyes will be on her and Jesus. Thank you, God, for my mother and thank you, Mom for showing me what a loving God looks like. Without your influence, this book would never have been written. – *J.W. Irvan*

My father was the most brilliant man I have ever known. Although he is no longer here on this earth with us, he remains the most brilliant man I ever knew. He was self-educated, read voraciously and wrote both fiction and nonfiction, as well as poetry. He told me, "If you want to be a writer, read." He was right, of course, and I did just that. He held the written word in the highest regard. He taught me there was power there. Power in the ability to communicate my thoughts, feelings and to instruct. He told me to write every single day. Something. Anything. Just write. He ignited my passion for writing when I was very young. Were it not for that spark, I certainly never would have completed a novel.

The other side of the equation is my mother. While Dad fostered the technical side of writing, it is my mother who laid the foundation for the content within these pages, as well as, the other books in the series. She is my spiritual rock, constant and unfailing; wise and patient. She taught me about love, tolerance, forgiveness and truth. She watched all her children wander away from God at different times but she prayed for us to find our way back. I know her prayers and petitions to the Lord for me are what brought me to a place of surrender and resulted in my desire to write about His perfect love. *– Cheryl Bills*

Professional Credits & References

<u>Artists</u>

DC Talk   Third Day

TobyMac

<u>Songs</u>

-Jesus Freak by DC Talk

-Everywhere You Go by Third Day

<u>Movies</u>

Sling Blade

Foreword

Storytelling has been around as long as humanity, predating written languages. Jesus was a master storyteller. His most profound truths were communicated through stories that captured the imagination and stuck in the memory of His listeners. The struggle between good and evil, between God and Satan, between the forces of light and the forces of darkness are also as old as humanity. Great story telling is a part of being human. And a part of being a Christian.

We are blessed to have high quality Christian literature available to us to read, enjoy, and be inspired, motivated, and challenged, while also being entertained and edified. There is no small amount of fiction literature available on the market today, Christian or not. And in general, not all fiction is equally interesting to every reader. Some like romance stories. Some like stories from bygone eras when life was simple and values more traditional. Some like sports stories where our heroes and villains are also talented athletes who seem bigger than life, except when their problems and struggles seem a whole lot like ours. Why another novel in the growing tradition of Christian fiction? Because stories need to be told in a way that will capture us and challenge us and inspire us. And that takes a unique ability and task that is not easily accomplished.

J.W. Irvan and Cheryl Bills are rising to the challenge of providing quality stories that reflect real life people who are struggling with everyday problems. The unique approach for Irvan and Bills is that they bring more to the story than just interesting character development and captivating plot lines. They also understand that there is more to reality than meets the eye. They understand that the forces of good and evil that play out in the hearts and minds of people are also the forces that wage war in a timeless, spiritual realm that spans all of human history. The struggles, the forces, the issues, the truths that are brought out in The Last Rose series reflect everyday life and yet are rooted in timeless truths from a Christian perspective.

Irvan and Bills portray their characters in a realistic way. The Last Rose series is not only great storytelling, it is also a message worth hearing and sharing with others. You will identify with the characters, their struggles, and their relationship paths that lead them to a greater understanding of not only themselves, but also of God's mission and plans for people. We cannot find God's plan for our life without others who assist and help us along the way. We need one another to be who God made us to be. And to overcome the challenges that life brings our way.

The Last Rose: No Mistakes is the first of this series of novels. The story moves at a good pace, and keeps the reader engaged. Taylor Stratton, Jack Anderic and Kate Abbot are an unlikely trio whose lives intersect for a purpose far greater than any of them can understand or see without the help of each other. Christianity has had its share of bad examples and failures through the years. The

Last Rose: No Mistakes and its sequels share part of that disappointing reality. But God's work is always bigger than the people who say they follow Him. The journey of faith and overcoming challenges and fighting the good fight means that you see the good, the bad, and the ugly in people and in yourself. The Last Rose: No Mistakes is the beginning of a great journey. You will find yourself caught up with the characters and see yourself in their life-story. More importantly, you may realize that your struggles and challenges are not unique to you, because you are also part of a bigger story: His Story.

Rick Adams

Special Thanks

From both of us, a huge thank you to our family and friends who quietly cheered us on for years. Your love and support has meant more than you can imagine.

— J.W. Irvan and Cheryl Bills

From: J.W. Irvan

My wife, Barb, has been extremely patient throughout this long process and I owe her a great big thank you. She is my very best friend, my lover, my biggest critic as well as my biggest fan. She makes our house a home and still makes my heart race after all these years. My Love, thank you for your support and your willingness to go with me on this wild and crazy ride called us. I love you.

Gloria Rovay and Gene Irvan. Big sis and big brother. Gloria taught me how to express myself at a young age and Gene shared my most intimate thoughts all through our youth. I'm still a work in progress but I owe a lot of my creating skills to both of you. Heartfelt thanks sent out to California and to heaven.

My pastor, Doug Corlew, is an amazing human being. Were it not for him, I wouldn't be where I am in my walk with Christ and the books in The Last Rose series wouldn't exist. His sermons are amazingly insightful and his work behind the scenes with the worship team (which I am blessed to be a part), is nothing short of anointed. However, it's his Christ-like manner that affects me the most. The quality of his character gives me a glimpse of a shadow of my beloved Lord Jesus. It is Doug's walk with God that has helped inspire me.

Finally, thank you Ted Dekker for taking me on all those amazing adventures and showing me what is Christian fiction.

From: Cheryl Bills

To my husband, Greg – thank you for encouraging me to go after my dreams, to grow and take chances. You supported this project and never once made me feel like I was neglecting you while I had my nose to the grindstone. You have a way of making me feel like I can do anything I set my mind to. I know that no matter what we go through that you always have my back. And you never let a day go by without making me laugh. I love you more than you know.

To Jane Harding, my high school English and Creative Writing teacher. You deserve recognition for the many ways you helped me hone my craft early on. But let's be honest, just having to endure my journals filled with teen angst, self-pity, self-loathing and whatever other dark shadows I managed to cast onto paper warrants a prize. The truth is, you made something I felt driven to do even more fun. You challenged me to venture outside my comfort zone and you held your ground when I pushed back. I got angry with you at times, but you had my respect above all else. You were just the right balance of tough and tender. As a teacher, you left your mark on me. As a woman, you inspired me. Thank you for sharing your gift with me.

To my spiritual leaders at Fielder Church, Jason Paredes (Pastor) and Reggie Scott (Worship Pastor):

Jason, you changed my negative opinion and softened my hard heart when it came to the entire church experience. A lifetime of bad experiences left me skeptical and jaded but you showed me what it looks like when a man comes before God with humility and vulnerability and leaves all he has at the pulpit. You beautifully portrayed how the supernatural is all around us, just beyond a thin membrane that separates this world from the heavenly realm. I love and respect the way you give so much of yourself every single Sunday. Reflecting on your words, I walk away from my church home each week with a renewal in spirit and fresh perspective. Without your honest teaching, I doubt I would have matured enough as a Christian to tackle something like writing this series of novels.

Reggie, you are immensely talented but there is so much more to you than that. Your humility coexists so perfectly with your energy and passion for The Lord that I am swept up in a transcendental experience when you lead worship. Music played a key part in my personal salvation so not surprisingly, you are continually connecting me to God in a way like no other. You should know, you inspired many parts of the first book and those to follow through things you've said and how time after time, through humble and unashamed worship, you ushered the Holy Spirit into the room for me to meet face to face.

To my friend, Kelley Farr - you seemed to be more excited about this project than anyone, possibly even myself and my brother. You were the first (and only) person to read the rough (very rough) draft of the first two books. You gave us honest and valuable feedback and you were our cheerleader all the way through the process. Your encouragement and excitement has meant the world to John and me. Did you ever doubt you would be acknowledged for your part in this? I love you, my sweet friend.

Last but not least, I must acknowledge Rick Adams, who I like to refer to as this project's Technical Advisor. When I say I couldn't have done this without you, you know I mean it! You put up with incessant questions and pestering. Not once did you ever make me feel like I was a bother and you never hesitated to share your wealth of Biblical knowledge with me when I asked. You are the most gifted teacher I have ever had the good fortune to study under. I cannot thank you enough for the time you put into this project to make sure I was staying as Biblically accurate as one can be when writing fiction. There is so much to speculate about in the Bible – so much we could just never know but when it came to the black and white facts, you always had the answers for me right off the top of your head. And when it was something to be interpreted, you were honest about all the possible paths that could be taken. Thank you for giving your time to this project. Thank you for never making me feel stupid and helping me understand things in the way that I can absorb. I imagine you chuckling at some of the crazy questions I threw at you. But you are a class act all the way. You always showed respect for my feelings and as a true teacher, you took me under your wing and imparted wisdom. I could have searched far and wide and never found a more suitable person to advise on these books. Nor could I have found one I respect as much as I respect you. I am so grateful for you, Rick, and for your prayers and your friendship.

Introduction

You shouldn't be holding this book in your hands. All the things that had to come to pass for this book to be written make its existence highly improbable. The fact that you are holding it now is testimony of how God never gives up on us.

First let's start with the fact that my arrival in life wasn't exactly planned. I think it's safe to say that with the 3 different forms of contraception that my folks were using and the fact that my mother was almost 40 years old, I beat the odds. Never mind that I have had so many close calls throughout my life, it's a miracle I am alive today. There is no rational explanation of how I survived some of these events that should have meant certain death, yet I didn't sustain so much as a scratch.

Second, my brother, John and I co-authored the books in The Last Rose series. You may ask, so what? Sibling co-writers may not seem unusual except for the fact that we're talking about two siblings that couldn't stand to breathe the same air for almost 20 years. It was only because of very different hardships in each of our lives during the same time period that we came together to form a friendship and establish the brother/sister bond when John was 29 and I was 19.

Not enough obstacles? What if I told you I was a self-proclaimed agnostic until I was in my thirties? Ah ha. The plot thickens, right? I am not proud of it, but it's true. I had nothing but contempt for Christians. I found them to be feeble-minded and weak-willed. They couldn't think for themselves. They blindly submitted to a fantasy that was based on some book. Oh, I was far too intelligent to believe in something that couldn't be proven scientifically. I was much too intellectually advanced

13

to fall for something I couldn't see or touch. I didn't even give God enough credence to hate Him. I simply said there was no proof He was real. Either way, I didn't care. I lived my life as if He didn't exist.

I was raised as a believer but at the age of 15, I turned my back on God. What I *deserved* was to be cast aside by Him and left to suffer the consequences. Forever. But that's not my story. God pursued me relentlessly and through a series of extremely unlikely events, I found myself drawn back to God in my early 30's. He got my attention, convinced me He was indeed real and I came to believe in God again. If you would have asked me back then if I was saved, I would have said yes. And I honestly thought I was, but I was wrong. How do I know? Because once I was truly reborn, it was an unmistakable transformation from the inside out.

The catalyst for this change was in 2010, when my brother, John, and his wife visited for summer vacation. He brought some CD's he thought I would enjoy. He asked me to listen to them and let him know what I thought. It was all contemporary Christian music, which I did listen to after he went back home. Some I liked, some I did not care for. There was one band, Kutless, that I enjoyed the most. But after listening to them a few times, the CD's were set aside and forgotten.

Fast forward a year to September 2011. My boss gave me permission to listen to music on my computer at work (with earphones of course), through Pandora. In case you aren't familiar with Pandora, it uses the information based on which selections you give a thumb's up (you like the song) to determine other songs and artists you might like based on the attributes of the song and artist you "liked". I was working with my earphones in and I noticed I was extremely agitated and angry.

Of course, there was no reason for me to feel this way. I racked my brain to figure out what had triggered me, but couldn't figure it out. The same thing happened the next day and the next. Finally, I realized it was the music I was listening to. It was dark and the lyrics were very depressive and mentally it had put me in a place of negativity and anger.

I switched my Pandora station to one of upbeat, pop music. The anger issue went away immediately. Pandora started taking my feedback (thumbs up or thumbs down) and began tossing in some random songs. One day while working and listening to Pandora, something I hadn't heard before started playing. I clicked over to see the playlist to find out who I was listening to and I saw the name of the artist: Kutless. My mouth fell open as I stared at the screen wondering how in the world Pandora had determined what I was listening before warranted putting Kutless into the mix. Nothing I found provided and explanation. Of course, now I know (pointing to the sky). Anyway, I liked the song so I gave it a thumb's up. Pandora took that and eventually other contemporary Christian songs found their way into my music playlist. By end of the following week, half of what Pandora selected for me was Contemporary Christian Music (CCM). By the end of the month it was all I was listening to.

It makes perfect sense that God would use music to communicate with me. Music had been a passion going back as far as I can recall. So yes, there was really no better way to speak to me. There I was, listening to song after song about forgiveness, redemption, God's love, freedom from the past, slate being wiped clean and they worked on me day after day after day. Little by little I was being broken.

As I was being broken, I was changing and becoming someone different. My new feelings were so perfectly expressed through these songs so I sought out more and more CCM artists and songs. I began reading my Bible and I understood it for the first time in my life. I couldn't consume the Gospel fast enough. I was so hungry for a true relationship with the Lord. Even though I knew who He was and what He had done, I had never made a real, personal connection with Him. I considered myself a Christian. I prayed and believed but apparently, I had not taken that crucial next step.

How could my soul be won by listening to music? It's simple, really. When I listened to these songs, I was intently focused on God. It was a deliberate and passionate focus on God's love, the price Jesus paid for me and how terribly unworthy I was. My mind was filled with musical testimony of God's love and with that I began to change inside. I was joyful for the first time in my life.

For months, I had that "off" feeling but at the time I didn't think much of it. Looking back of course, it makes perfect sense. In my mind, I see Jesus' presence on my doorstep marking the beginning of the surreal feelings I experienced. I imagine Him stepping up onto the porch the day that Kutless song played on Pandora. I think I had only given Him access to the front yard before that and I can't even tell you how much I regret that. But as I started focusing on Him, He remained on the stoop, you know – patiently waiting for me to open the door. His holiness in such close proximity was enough to make everything feel different than it ever did before. I can't tell you the date but I can remember how one day I felt like me and how gradually I started feeling like something was up. It took some time, but thankfully, the Lord is patient. I'm so glad He never gave up on me because one day the door opened and He stepped inside and BAM! Cheryl was a completely different person. My perspective on absolutely everything changed. I saw it all through new eyes. Things I used to enjoy and loved were repulsive to me. Things I had never dreamed I would do, think or feel became attractive and enjoyable. Then came the realization that I was truly free from the guilt, shame and poison of my past. I could shake off those chains and free myself because I was forgiven. My debt had been paid. I owed nothing. Wow.

It was New Year's Day 2012 and I was visiting friends in Austin with my husband. That morning I kept seeing my mother's church flash across my mind. I saw the building and the banner on the side of the building. I had driven by Fielder Church in Arlington for years and I knew my mother went there but I never gave it a second thought. But that day the images were persistent. At one point, I finally said out loud, "Okay, I get it. You want me to go to that church." And then the images stopped coming. It was as if God felt satisfied that I heard Him. I went to Fielder Church the following Sunday and attended the contemporary service. It has been 5 years now and I rarely miss a Sunday. It's not because I feel obligated. It's because I found my happy place where I am with like-minded people who love God and are unashamed. People who lift their arms in the air and weep openly - they don't care what other people think. These are the same people I once looked at with contempt when I was in rebellion. Now I am one of them.

I share that with you to say this. When I write about people who feel so far removed from God that they think He could never, ever love them, I am writing from experience. With all the hateful rhetoric I used to spew, God still loved me and still pursued me. He was tireless and relentless and He never gave up on me, even when I was most undeserving.

This book and all the books in the series are meant to glorify God, reveal His goodness and His faithfulness. The story is meant to reach into the mind and heart of the reader and resonate. It is meant to be a testimony as well as entertainment and here is why. What if by reading this story, a seed is planted that will someday take root? What if one soul that would otherwise be lost finds hope to cling to here and starts focusing on God? God will do the rest. But what if we can be part of that in some small way? My brother and I agree that this book was never about the people writing it - it's all about the person reading it. It's our offering. It's our attempt to be His hands and feet here on earth.

I started by giving you an idea of how unlikely this book could even exist, right? Think about all the things God orchestrated in order to position us perfectly for this project. Let me tell you how it got started. A few years ago, John started writing a story. He approached me in July 2014, asking me to proofread it, tidy up any errors and give him some feedback. I did as he asked and the following summer when he came for his annual visit, I handed it to him. I told him quite honestly, I didn't think it was in line with what he was hoping to accomplish, based on information he had shared with me. He asked me if I would be willing to help and I said I would. But then he took it a step further and asked me to write it with him. A collaboration? That was a huge leap of faith on his part. I was flattered but I wanted to be sure that was really what he wanted. He assured me he did. We scrapped the original story and started fresh in August 2015. By May 2016, the book was complete. John had a seed, I had some dirt and God brought the rain and this story wrote itself.

I hope this book and the rest of the books in the series make you laugh, cry, gasp, feel anxious, feel excited, think and fall in love with the people who live on the pages. I hope you read the last page of each book and want more. Most of all, I hope you are blessed in some way by reading the story of The Last Rose, because that is its purpose. It doesn't have to change your life or save your soul. Perhaps you are already a Christian and it simply takes you away to a place where you draw closer to God as you witness Him working in the lives of the characters. I never felt closer to God than I did when I was writing, because I was all about His business. I was immersed in His perfect love. I'm sure John would agree it was the same for him.

-Cheryl Bills

Part One

CHAPTER 1

Beatrice, the receptionist at County Behavioral Health Services, watched wide-eyed as the disheveled man stumbled frantically through the door and into her waiting room. Her finger was poised over the panic button underneath the desktop, ready to push if necessary. *Be professional. Be calm. Be alert.* She reminded herself then sat up straight, shoulders back and put on her brightest smile.

"Good morning! And how may I help you, Sir?" She asked with the same tone as a waitress greeting a customer with a pot of coffee in one hand and a breakfast menu in the other.

The man launched himself towards her, planted both palms down and leaned over the desk. "You can lock me up and throw away the key. That's how you can help me!" He panted. His dark brown hair looked like he had been in a wind tunnel. He wore a gray and black affliction tee shirt which was untucked over what looked like expensive designer jeans. His eyes were bulging mere inches from her face and she fought against the oncoming panic. This was all part of the job so she maintained composure, at least outwardly.

"Well, Sir we just need to get some information." She leaned back in her chair and reached to her right for the clipboard, never once taking her eyes off him. *Always maintain eye contact.* She mentally recited from the training she received less than a year ago. *Wait! Unless it was a certain type of patient then NEVER make eye contact!* Well, it didn't even matter at this point because she had already committed to eye contact. She was relieved when he straightened up and made an attempt to smooth his hair with his hands. *Whew. Now we're making progress,* she thought and took a deep breath. She grabbed a pen and slipped a fresh admission form onto the clipboard and stamped the date - June 2nd - at the top of the form. "Your name, please?" She asked. No way was she giving this man a pen to fill out his own forms. She could just see him stabbing her in the forehead with it.

"Taylor." He combed his fingers through his unruly hair, still trying to get it under control.

"Is that your first name or your last name, Sir?" She queried.

"Huh? Oh. Sorry. I'm Taylor Stratton." He looked around awkwardly as if just realizing what a spectacle he must be.

"Middle initial?" She continued.

"Really?" He leaned in again, but smiling this time, no bulging eyes. He was actually kind of attractive, Beatrice decided. His blue gray eyes were striking, with thick, dark lashes adding contrast. His nose gave his face its character. It wasn't wide but was only slightly bigger than average on profile. His bottom lip was full and pouty. Now that he had that crazy hair under control, it looked pretty good. It was thick and shaggy; not short but not really long either. He had some scruff on his face from not having shaved for a day or two. She estimated he was in his mid to late 40's and he stood about 6 feet tall with a very fit, muscular build which was obvious under the close-fitting tee shirt he wore.

He spoke again, snapping Beatrice out of her trance. "I come in asking to be locked up and we're seriously going to worry about my middle initial? Tell ya what…" He reached into his back pocket, retrieved his wallet and pulled out his driver's license. "…here, use this." He tossed the license onto the desk and it skidded across the smooth surface, over the edge and onto the floor next to her chair. For a moment their gaze held, frozen as if neither could believe that just happened. *I don't care how cute he is, he's going to kill me when I bend down for this thing. I just know it,* she thought as she leaned sideways over the chair's armrest to grab the license. She kept her eyes fixed on Taylor the entire time. Her stiff and awkward attempt to pick it up paired with the constipated look on her face made Taylor chuckle. Immediately the girl snapped upright with the license in hand. *Get a grip, for crying out loud,* she scolded herself.

"Have a seat over there, won't you Mr. Stratton?" She pointed to the bank of uncomfortable-looking waiting room chairs to her left. He saluted, pivoted on his left foot and walked away obediently. Beatrice copied down his information and decided that Intake could do the rest. She dialed extension 3473 and said "I have an 8-17" and hung up. That was code for a person that needed to be removed from the waiting room right away to complete paperwork elsewhere.

Marvin Petros, the Intake Coordinator softly cradled the phone after receiving the 8-17 from Beatrice at the front desk. The girl had a tendency to be overly cautious but that was not necessarily a bad thing in this line of work. He straightened the pens in the holder next to the phone and took a sip of coffee from his personal mug that boldly proclaimed "I Don't Do Mondays". Fortunately, this was a Thursday so off he went to retrieve his 8-17.

Taylor looked up when the door opened. A short, somewhat plump man with a severely receding hairline and small, round, gold rimmed glasses walked over to the receptionist. Taylor couldn't help but notice the collar of his light blue dress shirt was entirely too big around and his gray slacks were too long. Only the very tip of his black loafers was visible under the cuffs of his slacks which dragged on the floor behind his heels. He wondered if for some reason this man had to borrow clothes for work that day. *How could that even happen?* Taylor thought. *What could possibly make a man come to work in someone else's clothing?* He looked back over at the receptionist who was now whispering something to the man and then she pointed in Taylor's direction. The man glanced over and nodded. Taylor raised his hand and waved. The man's eyes widened a bit. *Was that wrong? Why did I wave?* Taylor silently admonished himself then reconsidered. What was he worried about anyway? He was trying to commit himself to a mental hospital. How could he mess that up?

"Mr. Stratton?" Taylor jumped at the sound of his voice. The man in borrowed clothes had approached while he was lost in his own inner dialogue. He handed Taylor the driver's license he had left with Beatrice. "I'm Marvin Petros. Would you follow me please?" Taylor followed Marvin down a short hallway into a small office. Marvin walked around his desk and sat. "Please make yourself comfortable, Mr. Stratton." Taylor took a seat in one of two faded mauve guest chairs across the desk from Marvin. The first thing he noticed was that everything was very neat and tidy. It was almost too perfect. All angles of every object on a given surface were in alignment with each other. The books on the shelves were in alphabetical order by author and papers on the man's desk were stacked perfectly. Even the man's coffee mug was lined up just so next to his phone and pen holder. "So, I understand you are requesting admission for treatment?"

23

"Yes please." Taylor answered politely.

"Were you referred here by your healthcare provider?" Marvin probed.

"No. I referred myself. After careful consideration, I found me to be unstable, delusional and unfit to function in polite society." Taylor joked but with a perfectly deadpan expression. *What? What are you saying, you idiot?* Taylor thought, completely shocked by the cavalier way he was responding to this very serious situation.

Marvin's mouth curved upward slightly. "I see. Well, you *appear* quite lucid." He leaned back in his chair, elbows on the armrests, clasped his hands and rested his chin on his index fingertips. *Hmmm. Poised like a classic shrink,* Taylor thought even though he knew the man was not a doctor or even a therapist. He was a paper pusher. But there were processes for everything and this was where he had to start.

Taylor leaned forward and looked Marvin in the eye. "Appearances can be deceiving, Mr. Petros. I think I need to explain why I came here."

"I agree, Mr. Stratton." Marvin smiled. "Can I get you something to drink before we begin? Coffee? Water? Soda?" He picked up his mug and stood.

"Water please. Thank you." Taylor replied. Marvin left the room briefly and returned with a fresh cup of coffee for himself and bottled water for Taylor.

"Okay, Mr. Stratton. Let's discuss what brings you here and then we can assess whether or not we can meet your needs." Marvin sat down and took a sip of coffee. "Start at the beginning whenever you are ready."

Taylor pondered for a moment then decided he should just start talking and pray that the impeccably neat and tidy Mr. Marvin Petros would be able to track along with him.

Chapter 2

Approximately three hundred twenty miles south of Taylor's hometown, Jackson Anderic pulled his '69 Chevelle SS into the parking lot of Rosie's Diner. He glanced at his watch - 12:00 pm sharp. He got out and leaned against the car breathing in the spring air. It was a beautiful day in Southern California. But no matter how perfect the day, he was a little nervous about talking to Danielle. After lunch today, everything would be different. Jack rehearsed some of the points he wanted to cover. First, today was the last day of May and they had been dating since February of the prior year, which was roughly 16 months and he believed they might be ready to take things to the next level. Second, he had accepted a position at Massachusetts General Hospital that very morning and would be relocating to start his new job on July 18th, which was six weeks away. Third, if they were going to keep seeing each other, she would have to consider going with him to Boston. If she wasn't, it only made sense that they part ways now. A long-distance relationship would never work for him.

Jack glanced at his watch. 12:06 pm and no sign of Dani. Where was she? This was not Jack's first time to climb out on a limb emotionally but it had been a very long time. The last time had been 7 years ago when he was ready to propose to his high school sweetheart, Stacy. That had been an epic fail. Since then he had been very reluctant to give his heart to anyone. Truth be told, he hadn't really given it 100% to Dani. He was still very guarded but they got along well and had fun together. It was an easy kind of relationship and there were not many demands or expectations. Likewise, there were no real conflicts or drama. Admittedly he and Dani weren't on the same page when it came to ambition in life or long-term goals but she was young and he believed that would develop as she matured.

Dani had just turned 22 and still lived with her parents with seemingly no desire to move out on her own. Jack was 27 and had lived in a few different cities before settling in at USC to get his Masters in Biomedical Engineering. Dani never went to college and was content to work the checkout counter at a local craft store. Jack was about to embark upon a career where his contributions would be instrumental in advances that would change people's lives for the better in the burn and trauma unit at Mass General. Dani had been working at the craft store since she graduated from high school and quite frankly had her hands full just figuring out how to key a 20% off coupon into the register. Would she be willing to leave mom and dad and step outside her comfort zone? Did she love him enough to consider it?

At 12:10 pm, Danielle eased her clunky Ford Escort in next to Jack's black Chevelle. She threw her car in park, typed something on her phone then tucked it away in her purse. After checking her lipstick in the rearview mirror, she killed the engine and got out. She smiled when she saw Jack leaning against his car. He was tall at just over six feet and had a wiry, athletic build – all muscle. He was wearing jeans, boots and a faded Radiohead tee shirt with a white button-down shirt open over top. The sleeves were rolled up a little bit. His short blond hair was stylishly spiked at the top with gel and looked perfect against his tanned face. His blue eyes lit up when he saw her and he smiled as he walked around the car.

Dani had been dating Jack for almost a year and a half but there was something about him that kept her forever banished outside his walls. She decided months ago that while he was a decent guy, he was not her *forever* guy. She saw herself with someone dangerous, unpredictable, maybe not such a good guy. She wanted someone rebellious. Jack was very nice and he was extremely grounded. He was responsible and kind hearted. Her eyes moved passed him to the car. She knew it was shallow but the truth was she would have moved on months ago if not for that car. She loved being seen riding around town in that black monster. How could the car look so dangerous and the owner be so safe?

"Hey Dani. Thanks for coming." Jack swept her up and lifted her off her feet a few inches. She was a petite 5'3" and light as a feather. He gave her a peck on the cheek before he lowered her back to the ground.

"Hi Jack." She kissed his cheek in return. "I only have an hour then I have to get back to work."

"After you, then." He opened the door and waited for her to go through before he followed.

The hostess led them to a booth near the back of the diner. Jack was happy about that as it gave a little bit of privacy. He was too nervous to eat a meal but ordered a slice of apple pie and a cup of coffee to keep him busy while Dani ate. She ordered a patty melt, fries and a glass of water. As they chatted, her cell phone vibrated on the table. She ignored it but it buzzed again with another incoming text almost immediately. She glanced at it but did not pick it up.

When their food arrived, Dani began eating immediately, while Jack put sweetener and cream in his coffee. He eyed his pie wondering if eating was in his best interest. His stomach was doing somersaults. He hoped the coffee would calm his nerves a bit.

"So, you sounded pretty excited when you called this morning. What's up?" She asked in between bites.

"Well, you remember when I went to Boston to interview for that job at Mass General?" Jack waited for her to acknowledge.

She had a mouthful but gave him a muffled "Uh huh" followed by a nod. Her behavior struck him as odd. She was a compulsive eater when she got nervous. Was she nervous now or just really hungry? Perhaps she suspected why he had asked her to meet him and she had a case of the nerves.

"They called this morning and offered me the position!" Jack raised up in his seat and put his hand out toward her for a fist bump. She hesitated to let go of her sandwich but finally did and gave him a weak brush of her knuckles against his.

"That's great, Jack. Happy for you." She replied without any real happiness in her voice. He suddenly felt deflated. Her reaction was so blasé.

Jack leaned in on his elbows and looked her in the eyes. "So, tell me how you feel about this, Dani."

She took the last bite of her sandwich and dabbed the corners of her mouth with her napkin. She was uncomfortable. Not only was the conversation making her feel uneasy but she may have eaten too fast. Or perhaps her patty melt wasn't cooked thoroughly. All she knew was her stomach was churning and she was breaking out in a cold sweat. She stared at the wall behind Jack.

"Dani? Are you listening to me?" He waved his hand in front of her face. She blinked and focused on him again.

"Yeah. I heard you." She ran her fingers through her short, dark hair. "This is what you wanted, right?" Tiny beads of sweat were forming above her upper lip. She took a long drink of water, hoping that would make her feel better.

"I didn't ask you how you thought I felt about it, Dani." He looked into her eyes. What was she thinking? And by the way, she was getting paler by the moment. If she was upset that he was leaving, this was the only thing that might be an indication.

"I'm not sure what you want me to say, Jack." She folded her hands on the table and sat very straight.

"Okay, let me be blunt then." He was no longer nervous, just annoyed. She was being evasive although he couldn't figure out why. "We've been seeing each other for well over a year, right?" He waited for a response. She nodded. "And I'm about to move across the country. I kind of thought you should feel something… sad that I'm leaving maybe?" He realized that for her to join him was no longer on the table.

"You just sprung this on me and I don't know what to say." Her phone vibrated again. She didn't even give it a look, but instead shifted nervously in her seat.

"Do you need to handle that?" Jack gestured towards her cell. "Someone seems awfully eager to reach you." He cocked his head to the side and raised an eyebrow.

"Don't worry about it." She waved her hand dismissively and changed the subject. "So, do you think your car will make it all the way to the east coast?"

"I'm thinking about selling my car." He replied matter-of-factly. "I won't need a car in the city. It would be a bigger hassle to try to find an affordable parking garage for it. Besides, driving in Boston? Fahgedaboudit!" He said with a thick New York accent, trying to lighten the mood. It didn't work. She remained distant and hard to read. Was she sad that he was leaving and playing it off so he wouldn't see her upset? Or did she really not care if she ever saw him again? The phone next to Dani buzzed again with another incoming text. That was four texts since they sat down in the booth. Maybe she should be taking them more seriously. What if someone was in trouble? What if there was a family emergency? By nature, he couldn't help but be concerned. "I really think you need to see if something is wrong, Dani." He pointed to the phone again.

"Fine, I'll check it." She snatched it up from the table and began scrolling through her texts. Her eyes widened and her mouth curved up with the faintest hint of a smile as she read. Jack could see by her reaction there was nothing upsetting in the texts – quite the opposite. She put the phone down on the table, face down this time. "Ellen wants to know if I can give her a ride." She dabbed her forehead with her napkin. "I'm going to have to go soon but before I do, tell me what you plan to do with your car. Do you have a buyer?" The girl was like a dog with a bone on the car subject.

"I haven't gotten that far yet. I mean, I just accepted the job this morning, Dani." He knew she had always had a thing for his car. In fact, the joke between them was she was only with him so she could ride around town in the car. Maybe it wasn't such a joke after all, he thought. Regardless, it seemed an odd thing for her to be focusing on. "Finding a buyer won't be hard. The car is mint."

"True. So…how much are you going to ask for it? There's a guy I know who might be interested." She was still pale but her eyes were suddenly alive with excitement.

"A guy? Who?" Jack felt his neck growing warm. This didn't feel right. He watched Danielle fidget in her seat as she picked at her fingernail.

31

"Huh? Oh… it's Ellen. Well not *Ellen* but a guy she works with, Dillon. He's looking for a car. I said I'd keep an eye out, you know. He *loves* old muscle cars." She said then grimaced. She meant to say Ellen *says* he loves old muscle cars. *Stupid!* She chastised herself. She held her breath for a few seconds. Maybe he didn't catch it.

"I see." Jack replied cautiously. "Well, I'm not 100% sure what I'm going to do as of this very moment. I have to say, I thought this was going to go differently. I had hoped…" He lifted his hands in despair. What was the point?

"Jack I'm not feeling well at all." She was starting to feel very queasy. "I'm guessing you thought I would want to follow you out there?" She laughed. "Yeah, *that's* not going to happen." She put her head in her hands. "Seriously Jack, I'm really not up for this." Then overwhelming nausea swept over her like a tidal wave. Her cell phone vibrated again.

"Maybe you should just…" Jack started speaking but she was up in a flash and darted off to the ladies' room with her hand over her mouth. "…text Ellen back." He finished.

As if on cue, the phone vibrated again. Jack grabbed the phone. Maybe Ellen needed more than just a ride. If Dani didn't want to deal with it, then he would. He swiped the screen and touched the text message icon. His heart felt like a stone in his chest when he saw the string of texts. None of them were from Ellen. For the past hour since they had met for lunch and sometime prior there were only texts to and from Dillon. The last one that just came in was like a blow to the solar plexus. Jack read each time stamped exchange.

*1:02 pm, **Dillon:** Just cut this loser loose already. You've wasted enough time in that stupid diner with him. Or do I need to come there and do this for you? Tell him it's over, baby. Or I will.*

His hand was shaking. *Not again*, he prayed. Jack scrolled back up to see where the string of texts began and started reading from there.

11:58 am, Danielle: I miss you so much! I can't wait until this is over and we can be together all the time. I have to meet Jack for lunch today but I'm going to tell him we're over and then I'll be a free woman! Woo hoo! Love you love you love you!

11:59 am, Dillon: I miss you too, Babe. Just get this over with as soon as you can and meet me at my place so we can celebrate. You called in sick to work today, right? Stomach flu or something like that?

12:02 pm, Danielle: Can't wait to see you. Yep, I told them I was contagious and barfing everywhere. LOL.

12:10 pm, Danielle: Just got to Rosie's. He's waiting for me in the parking lot. So ready to get this over with. Wish me luck.

12:33 pm, Dillon: How's it going? You break up with this idiot yet? LOL.

12:38 pm, Dillon: Are you okay? Is he giving you any problems, Babe? No way does it take this long to dump someone. Oh yeah, I wouldn't know, I've never been dumped. LOL!

12:53 pm, Dillon: Seriously, D, this is taking way too long.

1:00 pm, Dillon: I guess if you can't get out of there I need to give you some incentive. *inserted selfie of some young, skinny guy with long stringy hair and a goatee shirtless on a couch*

1:01pm, Dillon: *selfie again but this time he's flexing a pitiful excuse for a bicep while puckering like he's poised for a kiss*

Then back to the last one, which Jack had read first. So, Dani was not only cheating on him with some hippie but she was planning to break up with him today. Suddenly he felt stupid. He'd been cheated on before but that was many years ago. In fact, the last time he'd been serious about a girl, it ended because he caught her literally in the act of cheating which had been utterly devastating. As much as he cared for Dani, he wasn't nearly as emotionally invested as he had been with Stacy. This was more of a blow to his pride. How could he be so foolish? At least he had not gotten down on bended knee and asked her to join him in Boston so they could start a life together. Geez! How humiliating would that have been? He thanked God for saving him from that blunder.

Jack grabbed the ticket for $13.38 off the table and pulled a twenty from his wallet. He looked toward the ladies' room. Still no Danielle. It was time to end the suspense for Dillon. Jack typed: *He knows about us. He's history.* Then he pushed the send button and put the phone back where it had been before he picked it up. He took the ticket and the twenty to the front register and told the cashier to keep the change. Then he added, "Oh, and the girl who was with me is in the ladies' room. She isn't feeling well. Can you keep an eye on the table so no one takes her purse or her phone?"

"Sure will. You have a good day, hon." The cashier said cheerfully.

Chapter 3

Two weeks prior to meeting Marvin Petros, Taylor had been a normal, average 47-year-old man. He lived alone in Seaside, California in a charming 3-bedroom craftsman style home with a perfectly manicured yard. Every morning he got up at 6:00 am and ate the same breakfast of toast with strawberry jam and 3 scrambled egg whites before leaving for his job where he worked as a landscape architect. He and his partner, Greg Rios, had started their residential and commercial landscaping business 15 years ago and had become very successful with locations in Salinas, Monterey and the original in Seaside.

One night he went to bed that same normal guy and woke up the next morning a completely different man. There was nothing special about that Wednesday morning other than the fact that while showering, Taylor experienced a blinding headache that made him hug the wall of the shower to keep from falling over. He closed his eyes and saw nothing but red. His ears were filled with the sound of what seemed like a thousand voices whispering all at once. The words were hard to make out at first but finally it became clear that it was just two words repeated over and over. Find her find her find her find her.

When the episode ended, his headache and the red hue had vanished. When he finished his shower, his hands were shaking so badly he thought he might not be able to towel off. The drive to the office was uneventful although he was in a mental fog for most of it, still wondering if what happened in the shower had been real or imagined. Maybe he had a brain tumor. He'd have to get a PET scan, CAT scan, MRI or whatever you got to check for a brain tumor, he told himself. By the time he pulled up in the office parking lot he had talked himself out of the brain tumor theory. It had to be his imagination, right? It seemed best to put the whole thing behind him and get on with his day.

Taylor cheerfully greeted the staff as he made his way through the building to his partner's office. Greg Rios, Taylor's best friend since 6th grade and partner for over a decade and a half sat behind a large glass and chrome desk. Greg's taste was ultra-contemporary and sleek. Everything in his office screamed modern design. Greg himself was anything but sleek and modern at 5'10", 180 pounds. His thick, wavy jet, black hair complimented his café au lait complexion and big brown doe-eyes. He had a pencil thin mustache and a small scar on his upper lip from when he crashed his bike into a tree when he was 8. Greg always dressed in traditional old school businessman attire: lightly starched white long sleeved dress shirt, red power tie and black dress slacks with perfect creases running down the front of the legs. He looked up when he heard Taylor come in. "Top o' the mornin' to ya', Sire." Greg grinned. "What's on tap today, T-Rex?"

"Hey, Boss." Taylor plopped down in the black leather and shiny chrome chair across from his partner. "I have to work up a quote for a new client at 10:30. Then I need to follow up on that bid for the new high school in Watsonville. Until then I might return a few phone calls and answer some emails."

"I hear you, man. I have a few potential new accounts from yesterday afternoon to scope out." Greg patted a folder on his desk. "Hey listen, Renee and I were wondering if you wanted to come over for dinner tonight. She's making pot roast. I'm not going to lie, it will be terrible but I figure we can fake eat and feed the dog under the table when she's not looking. Then we say we need to make an ice cream run or something and grab a burger while we're out." Greg often extended invitations for dinner both out of a

36

desire to provide companionship to his widowed friend in addition to having someone to share the misery of his wife's cooking. It was a symbiotic arrangement in Greg's mind. He smiled expectantly at Taylor. "What do you say?"

"You know, while that is one *tempting* offer I'm going to have to decline this time, my friend. I haven't been feeling well and I think I might even head home early today." Taylor's face went pale at the memory of earlier that morning.

"Yeah, I didn't want to say anything but you don't look so good, T-Rex." Greg leaned forward on his elbows. "Rain check, then? But I'm warning you, I'm hitting you up next time she makes meatloaf. It's like a burned brick covered in watered down ketchup." He leaned back again, shaking his head. "I can't go through that alone, man. Not again." He shuddered dramatically which made them both laugh.

Back in his own office Taylor turned on his computer and checked email. He responded to all of them then picked up his phone to check voice mail. "You have one new message." The female computer-generated voice announced. "Message one…today at…2:12 a.m." Silence then music playing softly. Really? Someone called in wee hours of the morning and put him on hold so he'd have a Muzak message when he came in? Okay. Weird. But then he realized it wasn't even Muzak. It was the actual song and an old one, too. Bette Midler's voice made a haunting entrance. *"Some say love, is like a river that drowns the tender reed. Some say love, it is a razor that leaves your soul to bleed. Some say love, it is a hunger. An endless aching need. I say love, it is a flower, and you its only seed."* Taylor remembered the song but not the title. The harder he tried to remember the name of the song, the more his head hurt. His ears began to ring and his vision

37

turned to a red haze. Then the music faded and he heard whispering, this time a single voice. "Find her." Then click. The female computer voice was back, "To save this message press 1. To forward this message press 2. To delete this message press 3. To repeat this message press 4." Taylor pressed 4 with a trembling finger. "Message deleted." Lady computer voice announced. "What the…?!? I pressed 4, you wingnut!" He slammed the phone receiver down and pressed his fingertips to his temples and rubbed. "How is that even possible?" He moaned out loud.

"I was wondering the same thing." A voice came from outside his office door. "How can you have a headache when that huge melon of yours is so obviously empty?" Taylor looked up and saw his older brother, James standing in the doorway with his arms folded across his chest and a huge grin plastered across his face. Taylor quickly made his way from behind his desk and embraced his brother.

"Oh man! It's sure good to see you, Jay" Taylor patted his brother on the shoulder and invited him into the office. James took a seat and gave his brother a concerned look.

"Um… you okay, little buddy?" James cocked his head to the side waiting for an answer.

"I'm good. But I haven't had coffee this morning so I'm getting one of those caffeine headaches. I'll be right as rain once I get a java injection." Taylor stood up, smiling at his big brother. "Come with me to the kitchen and I'll buy you a cup."

They walked to the kitchen and each poured a cup of freshly brewed coffee, then sat down at one of the small round dinette tables. They chatted briefly about work and caught up on the latest news since the last time they spoke. James told Taylor he wanted to discuss the anniversary party in a few months for Mom and Dad. "I'll secure the venue if you think you can take care of finding her." James said. Taylor sat back startled by his brother's words.

"I'm sorry, what did you say?" Taylor gave his brother a suspicious look.

"I said, I'll secure the venue if you think you can take care of the caterer." James eyed his brother with concern. "What do you *think* I said?"

Taylor was immediately embarrassed. "I don't even remember now." He laughed nervously. "Of course I will hire a catering service. I know a couple of good ones."

"Great. I'll get with Matt and put him on finding us a band that plays those golden oldies. You know how Dad loves that big band stuff." James stood up to leave. "So we'll reconvene in a few weeks and see where we're at?"

"Sure, sure. Looking forward to it Jay." Taylor stood and began to walk James out. "This is a great idea for Mom and Dad. I just hope our baby brother can keep it a secret. You know how he is." Their youngest brother, Matt had a habit of spilling the beans anytime there was something covert in the works.

James chuckled. "I'll just threaten to break both his legs if he lets the cat out of the bag." He turned around when he got to the front door and gave Taylor a very somber look. "I love you, little buddy." He said.

"I love you too, Jay." Taylor smiled. "Hey thanks for coming by. Seeing you is just what I needed today."

James beamed at Taylor. "Think nothing of it. What kind of a brother would I be if I didn't stop by and tell you to find her?" He waved and was out the door.

****

Marvin finished scribbling something on his clipboard and looked at Taylor. "So, just to recap, what I am hearing is that you heard voices in the shower, heard a song on your voicemail and heard your brother telling you to 'find her'. Is that right, Mr. Stratton?"

"Yes. In a nutshell." Taylor replied. Marvin scribbled again. Taylor took a sip of water and recalled the rest of that week's events. On the second day he had decided it would be prudent to start keeping track of everything that happened. He bought a journal and began documenting events starting with the first occurrence on the first day. Then each day he made detailed entries about everything that had happened that day. There had been numerous, random headaches accompanied by the red hue and voices. A couple of days after the first episode in the shower, he had been in the grocery store picking up a few items when he could have sworn he heard the clerk come over the PA system and say "find her". In a panic, he ran up to a woman with a toddler in her cart and demanded she tell him what the PA announcement had been. She had looked at him like he had grown a second head and replied, "Um... price check?" Then she quickly whisked her cart and toddler as far from Taylor as she could get. He decided at that moment that interacting with the public was not the best idea and he should lay low and stay home over the weekend. He figured it would be pretty safe watching TV and reading, but he was wrong. While watching a crime drama, a commercial came on for laundry detergent. The name on the bottle of detergent was New and Improved Find Her. This was followed by a stabbing pain in his head and the living room was suddenly washed in red. He dropped the remote on the floor, stood up and went up to the TV for a closer look. By the time he got up close, it read New and Improved Ultra Clean. The pain was gone and the room looked normal.

"It's official, sports fans. Taylor Stratton has lost his pea-pickin' mind!" He announced to the empty room. "And the crowd goes wild!" He punctuated that by making the 'Haaaaaaaaa' sound to simulate a cheering crowd and threw his hands in the air in celebration. He turned off the TV and went to bed.

There were a couple of similar shower incidences again the second week, then more TV shenanigans. Finally, he stopped watching TV altogether. Then on Thursday morning, the worst one of all happened. He was working with a client on a quote for a residential job and was assessing the property so he could draw up preliminary plans for the client to review. The couple had gone inside the house while Taylor walked around the perimeter of the home taking measurements. They had a small white dog in the back yard on the other side of a short picket fence where Taylor was measuring. The dog saw him and started barking excitedly. Taylor leaned down to pet the Maltese who jumped and propped his front paws up on the fence, poised to be petted. He noticed the charm that hung from the dog's collar had RILEY engraved on it. As he patted the dog on the head, the Maltese began to howl happily. Taylor laughed. "Hey there, Riley. How you doin', boy?"

Riley jumped down and ran in circles a couple of times then returned for more petting. "Yeah, you like gettin' pettin's, don't you, Riley? You like that, huh? Yeah? What do you want, boy?" Taylor chuckled at Riley who looked like he was smiling. The dog howled again but this time he formed words. "Find herrrrrr!" Riley howled. Then again and again, he repeated urgently. It was unmistakable. Taylor was frozen where he stood for what seemed like an eternity. The couple came outside to see what all the noise was about just in time to see Taylor drop his tape measure and walk quickly to his car and drive away.

"And that was when I came here. I drove straight from that house to this place because I know for a fact that hearing animals talk is certifiably insane." Taylor uncapped the water and took a long drink.

Marvin wrote for a long time before he looked up at Taylor. "Okay Mr. Stratton. I have a good idea what you have experienced but your application has to be reviewed by our team before a decision can be made."

Taylor was astonished. "You can't lock me up?" He asked, feeling defeated. After a story like that, he was sure Marvin would fall all over himself to put him away.

"That's right, Mr. Stratton. You would undoubtedly benefit from therapy but you do not pose a threat to yourself or others which means we will not admit you on the spot." Marvin explained. "Go home, Mr. Stratton. Get some rest. And we'll call you when we can determine what course of treatment is best for you." He handed Taylor the clipboard with the patient information form on top. "Just fill out your contact information. Phone number, email, so we know how to reach you." Taylor wrote down all the information, still surprised that he was not being fitted for a straightjacket and escorted to a padded room.

Taylor left the County Behavioral Health Services building in a bit of a funk. He was exhausted from reliving the past weeks, not to mention the strain of the day itself. He didn't know what to do next. After searching for entirely too long, he finally found his car in the parking lot. He had been so frantic when he arrived that he paid no attention to where he was parking or how. He looked at his car now which was cock-eyed and taking up two spaces. It always annoyed him, when people parked like that and now he was one of them. *Oh, how the mighty have fallen*, he thought.

Since this whole ordeal had started, Taylor had prayed for God to make it stop. He prayed for peace and for release. He prayed that he wouldn't flip out in front of people that were important to him or hurt anyone or himself as a result of his diminishing sanity. But today when he was at the end of his rope, he prayed in a way he hadn't before.

"Father, I don't know why this is happening. All I can do now is ask what you want me to do. Please Lord, show me." He spoke out loud and loosened his grip on the wheel a bit, feeling his tension starting to subside a little. "You know what's going on with me. I trust you." And he meant it. He began to feel calm and peaceful for the first time in weeks.

He was stopped at a red light when Taylor had a quick mental glimpse of his church. It was like having a photograph waved in front of him for just a split second. That seemed odd but he had asked to be shown, hadn't he? It was Thursday. Somehow, he would have to survive the rest of today, all of Friday and Saturday and then maybe Sunday he would get an answer.

Chapter Four

Back at his apartment, Jack picked up a magazine, went out to the balcony, and settled into a comfy chair to read an article about nanotechnology. *A little light reading*, he thought and chuckled. From an early age, it was evident to everyone that Jack was intellectually gifted, but he had a creative side as well, especially when it came to music. He started taking guitar lessons when he was 6 years old and took to it like a fish takes to water. He could read music and play by ear, and by the time he was in junior high, he was an accomplished musician and songwriter.

Jack's mother and father had divorced when he was 3. Rebecca, Jack's mother had full custody of him but allowed her ex-husband, Chris, see him as often as he wanted. She felt it was important for a boy to have a relationship with his father in spite of whether or not the parents could live under the same roof. Regardless of his ex-wife's generosity, Chris wasn't as involved in his son's life as he could have been, so Rebecca did her best to take up the slack wherever she could. They went to church together two days a week, which is where he witnessed his mother serving others. She volunteered for everything from working in the preschool ministry to welcoming guests and handing out bulletins before service. As if that wasn't enough, every Sunday after church she stopped at McDonald's and bought several bags of hamburgers and she and Jack took them to an area on the way home where many homeless people gathered. Rebecca's compassion for others was genuine. Her active participation in church throughout the years, along with her kindness towards others in every facet of her life, impacted Jack who began serving in the youth ministry as soon as he was old enough. Jack loved God above all else. Music was the gift he shared and how he served.

After a half hour on the balcony reminiscing about his youth, Jack went back inside the apartment, grabbed another magazine, and settled into his recliner thumbing through it absently. Something caught his attention and he stopped on an interesting looking article about a man named Gilbert who decided to take time off and see the country – by bus. In the article Gilbert related his experiences - both humorous and harrowing - as he traveled all over the US by Greyhound bus. From the scenery to the eateries in the towns to the colorful passengers, the story captivated Jack. By the time he finished reading, he had made up his mind that he would leave earlier for Boston than planned and make the journey by bus rather than flying.

Fortunately, time was a luxury he had. The recruiter at MGH had already secured an apartment for Jack within walking distance of the hospital. It was fully furnished and all utilities including cable would be on when he arrived. Jack had been told to ship his personal belongings to the apartment where the recruiter would receive them and unpack for him. He sent an email to the recruiter and told him that he would be shipping his belongings this week and would be arriving somewhat earlier than expected but wouldn't know exactly when until the arrival time drew closer. Jack thanked him for all his help and promised to contact him when he was a day or so from arriving in Boston.

Jack was the kind of man who always played it safe. He had a plan for everything and then a backup plan for the original plan. As a rule, he did not like being unprepared. But for some reason the idea of setting out to start a new life with only a broad idea of "what, when and how" was suddenly very attractive. He had never really done anything spontaneous before. The more he thought about it the more he was convinced that this was exactly what he needed.

Chapter Five

Greg was out of the office Friday, so Taylor was able to work all morning in relative solitude. He remembered he had promised his brother he would handle catering for their parents' anniversary party, so he called and made arrangements during his lunch hour. Once he had confirmation that everything was all set, he emailed the details to James. Afterwards, he called the County Behavioral Health facility to follow up on his admission status. The woman on the other end of the line could not find any information on him in their system.

"Taylor Stratton." He repeated. "I filled out the application completely. Maybe you can check with Mr. Petros."

"I'm sorry, Mr. Stratton, you said Petros?" The voice on the other end sounded confused.

"Marvin Petros. Little fella in big clothes? Looks like George Costanza from Seinfeld? He's the Intake Coordinator I think." Taylor heard the sound of papers being shuffled around and then the voice asked to put him on hold. He waited a few minutes then she came back on the line.

"Mr. Stratton are you sure you called the correct facility?" She asked.

"Uh, yeah." Taylor paused. "Yes, I'm sure. You're located across the street from a flooring warehouse, right?"

"Yes. That's correct." She seemed to have run out of excuses, he thought. Maybe she was new.

"Okay so, is Mr. Petros there today? I can come in and speak with him in person." Taylor offered.

"Well the problem is there is no Marvin Petros here. We have several Intake Coordinators but they are all female." She told him.

"I'm on my way." Taylor announced and hung up the phone. He was out the door and in his car 5 minutes later.

He entered the facility and yes it was the same place. He walked up to the front desk where Beatrice sat engrossed in something on the computer. She glanced up then back down then back up again smiling brightly. Did she remember him? Of course, she did, Taylor thought. They always remember the weirdos.

"Good afternoon, Sir. How may I help you?" Beatrice folded her hands on the desk in front of her.

"Hi again." Taylor flashed his most charming smile. "I'd like to speak with Mr. Petros if he has time. He was looking into something for me and I need to find out where we're at on it. If he's not too busy, of course." He shoved his hands into his pants pockets and rocked back on his heels, still smiling. Beatrice wanted very much to oblige but there was just one problem. He was asking for the impossible. He wanted to see someone who didn't exist, at least as an employee of this facility.

"I'm sorry, Sir. I remember you coming in yesterday but if I recall you left before seeing anyone." Beatrice's brow wrinkled as she spoke. "Did someone contact you later that day?"

"Okay, I'm confused. I clearly remember you called Marvin Petros out and gave him my paperwork. I went back to his

47

office and spoke with him for over an hour. Are you telling me you don't remember all this? That was just yesterday." Taylor said.

"No sir. I'm telling you we don't have anyone here by that name and I remember you very clearly. You sat for 10 or 15 minutes then told me you couldn't wait any longer. You said you had to go find her and you walked out." Beatrice recalled the conversation.

Taylor felt the room spin and his legs started to buckle. He apologized and rushed over to a chair and sat. Beatrice came out from behind her desk, walked over to the water cooler and filled a cup. She kneeled down by Taylor who was sitting with his elbows on his thighs and his head in his hands.

"Here. Have some water and take as long as you need." She touched his shoulder. He turned towards her, his face contorted. How could this be happening? He couldn't possibly have imagined Marvin Petros and the entire session he had with the man in his office. It just wasn't possible. "Is there someone I should call, Sir?" Her hand was still on his shoulder. Her compassion was genuine and he was grateful. He smiled weakly and took the cup of water.

"No, I'll be okay. I just need a moment if that's alright." Taylor said quietly. "Thank you for the water, Miss." She nodded and returned to her desk. While Taylor tried to regain his composure she glanced over periodically to make sure he was doing alright. *What must she be thinking about this?* Taylor wondered. But he knew. She dealt with troubled people every single day. She was thinking he was nuts, what else? At least she wasn't terrified of him like she was the day before. Or had that even happened? He wasn't sure anymore what were memories and

48

what were delusions. One thing was certain, he wasn't going to get any help here. He pulled himself together then drove back to the office to finish out the work day.

About an hour before closing his new email message alert sounded. He closed the browser and clicked over to his Inbox. He blinked several times certain his eyes were deceiving him. He wished he had someone else there if only to validate that what he was seeing was real. New Message from MARVIN PETROS. Taylor looked around the room suspiciously before clicking on the email. "So, my imaginary friend is sending emails, huh?" He said as he leaned forward to read the email from Marvin.

> *Dear Mr. Stratton,*
>
> *I realize you are confused by now after attempting to follow up with a man no one remembers. I cannot offer you a thorough explanation but I can tell you that being locked away in a mental health facility would be in direct conflict with The Plan and simply cannot be allowed. Go to church on Sunday and I promise at least some of your questions will be answered.*
>
> *Yours Truly,*
>
> *Marvin Petros*

Taylor must have re-read the email a dozen times. He tried printing it, for proof that it was real, but the paper came out blank each time. There was really nothing else to do but go to church on Sunday and wait for something to happen there.

The service Taylor attended each week was held in a very large auditorium in one wing of the church building. It was so large in fact that there were several jumbo television screens placed so everyone could see the speaker well.

The band usually came on stage and started to warm up about 5 minutes before service was to start. It was a contemporary service so the music was the same as what played on contemporary Christian music radio stations. There were four worship leaders who rotated each week. His personal favorite was Robbie, a young African American man who was very charismatic and talented. When he led worship, it was electrifying. He got everyone pumped up and Taylor felt the Holy Spirit moving through the crowd with vigor when Robbie led. Taylor wished he could have joined the church band. As the drummer in a band in his teens, he had a passion for music. He was good on the drums but he dreamed of being great. Every week he sat in his usual seat and had the same fantasy.

The drummer did not show up for some reason and the staff had to scour the congregation for a substitute drummer. Of course, Taylor would volunteer to help them out of their little jam "just this once" and then proceed to blow the crowd (and the fellow band members) away with his amazing skills. Afterwards they beg him to be their regular drummer permanently, promising to keep the old drummer as backup in case Taylor ever got sick or needed to take a Sunday off for some reason. It was the same imaginary scenario every week and it always made him smile.

This morning the band came out and warmed up as expected until one of the staff members got up on stage and welcomed everyone and announced the subject matter for the sermon, "When God Calls, Will You Answer?" He stepped down and the band started playing. Taylor stood with the rest of the congregation throughout the set of three songs. All were particularly impactful and spoke to his current state of mind. It was good to be reminded of God's unfailing love and compassion. Whatever he was going through, he wasn't alone, never alone.

The band stopped and the intro film started which marked the official beginning of the sermon. Pastor Justin placed his water bottle and Bible on the podium. Justin had an easy, laid back style and came across like he was having a one on one conversation with you. He talked about his call to ministry and how being a pastor was the last thing he ever expected to be. He injected plenty of humor, as usual, then he got into the meat of the matter. He spoke of being connected and hearing God when he calls you to His purpose. Scriptures went up on the mega screens as Justin read from Colossians. Taylor read along but something was wrong with the slide on the screen. He watched as the words literally fell from the sentences and the letters landed in a heap on the floor of the stage. Blank screen. Taylor shifted in his seat and looked around. No one seemed to notice that something was amiss. Was that possible? Was no one else looking up there? He studied the crowd. Plenty of people were looking at the screens but didn't seem to think anything was wrong. The screens went red and white letters emerged slowly and came into focus.

ONLY YOU CAN SEE THIS.

Taylor felt heat rushing up his neck and over his face. It was happening again. God help him! The words faded and were replaced.

YOU PRAYED FOR ME TO SHOW YOU WHAT TO DO.

He felt the sweat beading along his brow as he surveyed the audience again. No one else seemed to be seeing this. He was crazy and his insanity had followed him to church.

NO, TAYLOR. YOU ARE NOT INSANE. I AM CALLING YOU TO DO IMPORTANT WORK. WILL YOU ANSWER?

He blinked twice and the words never went away. The question mark was blinking. He swallowed hard. "Yes. Tell me what to do." He whispered. The woman in front of him turned her head slightly as if she thought he was talking to her.

ONE OF MY CHILDREN IS LOST AND HAS BEEN LIED TO BY THE ENEMY. SHOW HER THE WAY TO ME AND PROTECT HER FROM THE EVIL ONE.

Suddenly Taylor was terrified.

HE WILL USE DECEPTION AND OTHER METHODS TO DISCOURAGE YOU. ONLY YOU WILL BE ABLE TO FIND HER. COUNTLESS SOULS HANG IN THE BALANCE.

What in the world made God choose him? As if he was up to challenging Satan over anything. He wasn't equipped to handle the forces of evil. Plus, he did not know who he was looking for or where to find her.

TRUST ME AND I WILL PROVIDE EVERYTHING AND EVERYONE YOU NEED. YOU WILL TRAVEL EAST AND I WILL GUIDE YOU ALONG THE WAY. NO LONGER QUESTION YOUR SANITY. IT IS I WHO SPEAKS TO YOU IN YOUR MIND AND THROUGH THOSE AROUND YOU. PAY ATTENTION, LISTEN AND STAY ON THE PATH.

He prayed he would be able to find the faith and courage he needed to do what God was asking him to do.

YOUR FAITH GAVE YOU STRENGTH WHEN YOU THOUGHT YOU COULD NOT GO ON EVEN ONE MORE DAY. YOU HAVE THE FORTITUDE TO COMPLETE THIS TASK. DO YOU BELIEVE?

Without hesitation Taylor, said aloud, "I believe!" Heads turned towards him and there were a few chuckles followed by clapping.

"Amen to that!" Justin agreed. Taylor could only surmise that his outburst had somehow fallen into place as an appropriate response to something Justin had said. *Thank you for that, Lord.* Taylor thought. And then he prayed, who am I looking for? How will I know when I find her? Will you give me a name? An address? Something? He looked up at the screen which was now white and blank. A tiny red dot in the center began to emerge. The image spun slowly as it began to grow and unfold. In a split second the memories came rushing back. He remembered the song playing on voice mail and how each time he saw this very same color of red when his head began to hurt. Now in the middle of the screen was a tiny rose bud which very slowly blossomed into the most breathtaking image he could ever recall seeing. The beauty of it made his heart ache and his eyes fill with tears. He felt crippling sorrow and unspeakable joy all at once and he thought it might rip his heart from his chest. A single drop of dew cascaded down the petals of the rose much like a tear flowing down a cheek. Then two words appeared as the rose vanished like a mist. …FIND HER.

Chapter Six

Jack felt good about his newfound spontaneity. He crossed the room and grabbed an atlas from the bookcase, removed everything from the coffee table and opened the book. He would leave LA and head to… he slid his finger along the map and stopped on Utah. He had plenty of time since he didn't start the new job for 6 weeks and there were ample available funds thanks to savings and a generous sign on bonus from the hospital. The fact that there was no pressure to rush and be somewhere at a specific time made Jack giddy. Time to soak everything in and maybe have a memorable experience or two.

First things first, he made a call to his apartment leasing office and let them know the apartment would be empty the following week, even though the rent was paid through the end of July when his lease term ended. Next, he decided he better start getting his belongings boxed up and ready to ship to Boston. Finally, he called his friend John and told him the schedule for vacating the apartment had changed. John had previously agreed to take on the task of storing Jack's furniture until it could be sold. Jack called him to let him know the timeline had moved up. John agreed to help move everything on Saturday. The weekend came and went fast with a lot of hard work but also some fun mixed in. Jack crashed on John's couch over the weekend and Monday morning he was on the 7:20 am bus from LA to Salt Lake City.

Chapter Seven

"So, this is solid?" Mary looked at Cassian soberly. He nodded and handed her a thick file.

"Why do we bother with this?" She took the folder and flapped it at him.

"Why do you ask so many questions?" He leaned back in his high-backed leather chair and continued. "And yes, it is confirmed. There was a great deal of sudden angelic activity around the primary subject which sparked interest. So, we began to gather intel on him. I have to give credit where it is due, though. He has done most of the work for us by keeping a detailed journal. Additional leads concerning the other subjects are based on information received from a psychic. Of course, that only goes so far. We don't know when, where, or how but we have clues that led us to who. It's a start."

Mary's expression revealed her skepticism of the use of psychics. What was next, a series on TLC called 'Cass and The Psychic Friends'?

"As far as the target is concerned, we do know that only the primary subject will be able to identify her. We need him to lead us to her." Cassian concluded.

Mary sat down in the easy chair across from Cass' oversized mahogany desk and looked around. His office was ridiculous. It was the purest form of exaggeration and cliché. Rich leather, dark glossy wood, finely carved and antiques as far as the eye could see. He even had a brass pole in the corner behind his desk with the American flag hanging from it patriotically. There were times this place made her nauseous with its absurdity. Other times, she accepted it for what it was, a very convincing façade.

Likewise, Cassian himself was the embodiment of the political cliché. By all appearances he was a thirty-something year old white protestant male – a product of Harvard Law who masterfully worked his way up the ranks to the position he now held. His light brown hair was very short and he was clean shaven. He was tall and fit and considered quite handsome. His steely grey eyes were provocative and could be hypnotic. He had a politician's smile, the result of expensive orthodontics and a lot of practicing in the mirror to perfect the desired effect. Today he wore a tailored grey pinstripe suit and oxblood shoes. He sat behind that regal desk, presumably handling national affairs –an illusion that was carefully crafted and well-executed. The reality was something quite different and only Mary was privy to what lay beyond the smoke and mirrors.

"I shall now open the file and read the dossier, Sir." Mary said in an exaggerated formal business-like tone and opened the file with grand gestures. If Cassian was amused, he gave no indication. She looked at the file which contained photographs and biographies on the subjects. "Shall I assume there are additional copies for me to disperse to my team?" She asked, then added with a sour tone. "Oh, if I may trouble you with yet another question, that is?"

"Your disagreeable nature is one of your finer qualities, Mary." Cassian pointed out. "And yes, I have four additional files for your team members." He stood up and walked around to where Mary sat. Pointing at the first page of the file he said. "Taylor Stratton is the primary subject. Everything you need to know about him is in that file. As I stated earlier, he is confirmed. Flip over to the next one." He directed and waited for her to get to the next one. "This is Jack Anderic, secondary target. Not confirmed but suspected so we treat him as if he is confirmed until we learn otherwise. Keep going." He made a circular motion with his hand as she turned pages. "Next is Katherine Abbot."

"I can read, Cass. But thanks for assuming I am completely inept." She said impatiently.

He dismissed her remark and continued. "Katherine is a wildcard. The psychic strongly suggested she is worth watching although nothing we have found out about her indicates that could be remotely true. Again, we err on the side of caution." He tapped the file with his finger. "We used conventional means to dig up background information on each of them. You can draw your own conclusions."

"Fine. Are we eliminating the subjects or…" She was cut off before she could finish.

"Absolutely not!" Cassian interrupted her. "We need Stratton alive because he is the only one able to identify the target. No one can be eliminated until the target is secured by us. I need you on Stratton right away, observing unseen, and if necessary you may interact, but keep it subtle. The last document in there contains the details of your mission, parameters, expectations, exclusions, etc. It is lengthy and detailed but since you are able to read as you so tactfully pointed out, I'll spare you the narrative."

"How gracious of you." She smirked. "Don't worry your pretty little head about this, Cass. I am capable of handling far more important missions that this, I assure you." She stood up.

"Sit down, Mary." Cassian said sternly and she obeyed. He hovered over her. "Once you read that last document, you will understand *this* is one of the most important missions you will ever have. There is a lot at stake and failure is not an option. We have to handle this with tact and discretion. Have I made myself clear?"

Mary stood, her face now within millimeters of Cassian's. She pressed forward into him and pushed. He backed up a step. *That's right,* she thought. Then she reached over, took the other four files from his desk and stuffed all five into her briefcase.

"I will be in touch." She said and walked out.

In the reception area, anyone watching would have seen a lovely young blonde woman in a brown pencil skirt, white silk blouse and 4-inch brown and gold Valentinos walking with an air of professionalism from Cassian's office. They would presume she had attended an important meeting that had to do with matters of national security. Her perfectly styled hair and flawless makeup would have distracted them from the fact that she gripped her briefcase so hard her knuckles turned white and the leather on the handle was beginning to blister beneath her hand. The cool, attractive exterior betrayed what lay beneath. No one saw what was seething just below the surface but her green eyes had turned a brilliant yellow and were ablaze as she waited for the elevator. Once inside, the cameras crackled and went dead as her flesh fell away and what lay beneath emerged and raged inside that tiny moving box. It sounded like a pack of wild dogs were fighting to the death inside the elevator as it moved from floor to floor, failing to stop for those waiting. The sound subsided by the time it reached the ground floor and the cameras began to function correctly once again. The doors opened and Mary stepped out as lovely as the day is long. She smiled at the security guards as she passed them on her way out of the building.

"Have a good one, Hank. Jim." She said with a wave of her free hand.

"Take care, Mary." They replied, watching her glide through the door.

She felt better after she was able to vent in the elevator. Her

59

relationship with Cassian was complex to say the least. They had been together since time on earth began, countless ages ago. In fact, they were together before that but she did not like to unpack those memories very often. She and Cass existed as angels before Lucifer and one-third of the angels were expelled from heaven. She was among the fallen although she could not clearly recall the moment where she made the choice to side with Lucifer in the act of mutiny.

From the time of the fall the pecking order was Satan (who Lucifer became known as after he was stripped of his heavenly position as a cherubim), then Cassian and Mary who had been paired with him. She thought the term "saddled" was more fitting than "paired" but who was she to split hairs? Her main job seemed to be do all Cass' dirty work and create a barrier between him and the rest of the demon population. She had to keep countless demons in line as well as managing the humans who were in her employment. The way she looked at it, she did absolutely everything and all Cass did was sit in a cushy office and play politician all day while deciding what to bother Satan with and what could be handled by Mary. Needless to say, Satan did not get bothered much at all. She did not even want to speculate what *he* did with his time.

The reason for Mary's anger today was the fact that once again she was treated like a rookie who needed to be spoon-fed information and walked through what to do. She wasn't new – this wasn't her first day. So why did Cass' pompous, smug attitude come out every time there was a task to be completed? She thought he took his human role far too seriously and had adopted the macho, chauvinist persona he saw in the men who surrounded him in D.C. Did he not realize that without these meat suits he would not stand a chance in a physical battle against her?

Was that an ambitious statement since he was superior in status and the only demon that reported directly to Satan himself? She knew for a fact it was not, but *how* she knew that was a mystery.

She approached her car and the driver took her briefcase, opened the door for her and handed it back before closing the door. She took the file out and decided to acquaint herself with the subjects before reading the mission directives.

She started with Taylor Stratton. A photo was attached to the biographical information for each of the three subjects. She unclipped Taylor's photo and memorized his face before reading his bio. She did the same with the next two subjects. Finally, she pulled the mission and directives from the file and read carefully. Cass was not wrong when he said it was important business. If the powers that be wanted to be safe, they would want the target identified for elimination. However, if Taylor's mission fizzled out before it got going then the target was no imminent threat. Her first order of business will be to try to discourage Taylor from embarking on his mission at all. Heading it off at the pass means crisis averted, everyone is satisfied and Mary gets another feather in her cap. She looked back at the first directive. It lined up with her plan and she was ready to proceed. Let the games begin.

Chapter Eight

Later Sunday afternoon Taylor sat on his front porch watching the neighborhood children play in the street and reflected on the morning. That had been a powerful message and while these things don't happen every day, he knew that everything he experienced today and over the previous two weeks had been very real. So it turned out he wasn't crazy after all. God had been reaching out to him all along and he was so wrapped up in himself that he never saw it for what it was. God finally had to come at him in a direct manner and He pulled no punches with the words on the mega screens. Taylor had been called and when you are called, you go where you are told and do what you are told. *So, I'm going east to find someone named Rose, I guess.* Taylor thought and closed his eyes. The image of that magnificent flower was etched on the inside of his eyelids. Every time his eyes were shut he saw it. Its impact defied description.

God's message had said everything and everyone he needed would be provided. Did that mean others were called to help find her too? That would be an interesting conversation starter, he chuckled as he imagined meeting someone for the first time. 'Hi. I'm Taylor. I'm on a mission from God to find one person in this whole world and all I know is she's east of here and her name may or may not be Rose. Are you also on a mission to find this mystery girl?' Big smiles and handshakes are exchanged and the reply of 'Why yes! Yes, I am! However, did you know? Let's join forces and get this done!' And then they hook arms and skip down the yellow brick road together. Taylor sighed.

But truthfully, he got the feeling this wasn't something he would return home from. In fact, Taylor had a strong feeling that surviving was a long shot. The forces of evil were going to be aligned against him, but God had promised he would give him everything he needed. All that was required was to believe and be obedient. In a nutshell, stay out of God's way and let Him do His thing. So here he was, Taylor Stratton destined to become a tool used by God for a specific and important purpose. However, he couldn't just walk away from everything and everyone without an explanation. Family and friends would have the authorities out looking for him everywhere because everyone knew Taylor just wasn't the type to take off and disappear. That being said, he needed to make arrangements, notify people and he would need money for this journey east. He had no clue how long he would be gone or how far he had to go. East could be east coast of the US or east as in another continent. The only plan was to go and keep going until God told him he was there.

This is actually kind of exciting if you think about it, Taylor told himself. *It's not every day an average Joe gets tasked with something this important. This is Old Testament stuff right here!* The idea made him smile. He imagined himself in a robe with long, flowing white hair, the way he pictured Moses. He stood holding a rose in each hand. *'Behold! I give you these two roses!'* Then his smile faded as he realized how much he had to do and how little time he had to prepare. There was little time to waste, but he stood on his porch for the longest time wondering just where to begin.

Taylor spent the rest of Sunday afternoon and early evening calling his family and friends to let them know he was going to take a vacation – a road trip across the country. Everyone thought that was an excellent idea since Taylor was the typical workaholic and rarely took time off. He spoke with his brother Matt and asked if he would be willing to house sit. Matt enthusiastically agreed. Taylor advised he would need to pay bills as per the spreadsheet that would be left for him. Most everything was on auto pay online, but just in case some random bill came in or something went hinky with the online system Matt would have full access to all accounts.

Once everything was squared away with the family, he called on a few neighbors to let them know he was going out of town and his brother would be house sitting while he was away. He gave them Matt's cell phone number in case they needed to reach him for any reason. Taylor went to bed that night thinking about how to wrap things up at the office the next day and prepare to leave this old life behind.

Chapter Nine

The bus station was a throwback to an earlier time, complete with the greyhound dog perched on top of the tall BUS sign that reached for the sky atop the vintage looking building. The inside left a lot to be desired, but Jack was not looking for luxury, he was looking for an experience. Looking around he couldn't help thinking he was the only one looking forward to boarding the bus. Most of the people milling around the terminal looked just that…terminal and like they had lost their will to live. Maybe this wasn't going to be the greatest mode of transportation. On the other hand, it was all about attitude, right? Jack couldn't shake the feeling that he was about to embark on something memorable.

He purchased his ticket for Salt Lake City and waited with his backpack, duffle bag and his guitar case in tow. Once he got claim tickets for his stowed bag and guitar case, he and his backpack settled in for the ride. Jack felt prepared for the long journey with his cell phone, headphones, snacks, water and various books and magazines.

The seat next to him was empty until Las Vegas at which time his neighbor was a young woman traveling to Salt Lake to see her cyber boyfriend. Visions of the MTV show Catfish filled Jack's mind as the girl chatted freely about her year-long online romance with Brayden. Her name was Hailey and she was 23 years old. Brayden was 34. She told Jack that Brayden was shy and afraid she would judge him by his looks if he sent any photos. He wanted her to love him for who he was inside, which she swore she did. Ironically, Brayden had no qualms about loving Hailey for what was on the outside as well as inside. He had requested pictures of her within minutes of "meeting" her in a chat room. Warning alarms and red flags were flying all over the place for Jack but Hailey seemed to take it all in stride. He listened politely while she told him all about Brayden and the plans they had made to get married and have a family someday. Jack wondered if she would like Brayden's other 3 wives as much as she liked Brayden. He chastised himself for being so callous and stereotyping but it was hard not to be suspicious when everything about this girl's situation screamed that something was wrong with Brayden. Finally, he asked her how Brayden had responded to the news that she was coming to see him.

"Oh, I haven't told him. I'm surprising him!" Hailey giggled with excitement. Jack felt his heart fall. Poor girl. This was going to be a disaster.

"Wow." Jack smiled. "So, if he isn't home or has something going on and can't put you up, you have money to get a hotel or something, right?"

"Of course." She assured him. "I wouldn't stay with him anyway. It's better to be cautious. After all, I don't really know him that well." She admitted. Jack felt relieved that she had a better head on her shoulders than he had first suspected.

"Smart girl." He said and winked. She smiled and started texting someone. Jack turned his attention to the scenery passing by outside his window. He was starting to see those landscapes that you always see associated with Utah but photos simply couldn't do it justice. It was breathtaking. They stopped in St. George where no one disembarked and a few new passengers came on board. Jack took advantage of the stop, got up to stretch his legs and look around. The world seemed bigger here than it did back home. The sky was wider and there was more earth to see. The bluffs were beautiful. It was a perfect example of God's artistic mastery. He went inside a little shop and used their restroom before he bought a couple of postcards and headed back to the bus. He settled into his seat, looked for Hailey, but she was gone. Finally, she ran up alongside the bus and got on with a huge grin on her face.

"Bet you thought I was going to get stranded here, didn't you?" She panted. The bus driver did a quick survey of the bus, closed the doors and they were in motion.

Jack watched the world go by outside his window. The trip to SLC was already worthwhile. He made a friend the first day of his new life. A friend who was probably going to be in a fetal position in the corner of a cheap motel room crying by midnight because the love of her life was a fraud. Perhaps he should be more optimistic. Maybe Brayden was exactly who and what he had represented himself to be. Maybe he was a nice man who just wanted to be loved for who he was and not how he looked. But more often than not these things didn't end well. Poor Hailey was so young and trusting. He prayed that she was in no real danger and that if she had to be disappointed that it would be as gentle a blow as possible. He tapped her shoulder. She opened her eyes slowly.

"Take my number. In case you end up needing anything after you get to Salt Lake." He told her. She opened her phone and put his name in as a new contact and his number. She called his phone so he would have her number and know it was her if she called. He added her as a contact as well.

Hailey took the gesture for what it was, a kind person who was looking out for her well-being. She had not encountered many people like Jack. She knew there was something different about him shortly after they had started talking. He never hit on her or made her feel stupid. He was *respectful*. There was not a lot of that in the world these days. Most people were after something or they just didn't care enough to acknowledge you were there.

"Can I ask you something?" Hailey pulled her headphones down and let them fall to her shoulders.

"Shoot." Jack turned and gave her his full attention.

"You are not like most men." She started.

"That's a statement, not a question." He observed.

"Ha. Ha." She poked his arm. "My *question* is, why? Why do you care what happens to a perfect stranger?"

"First of all, it's true. You are *stranger* than most people but you are *not* perfect." He teased and laughed when she rolled her eyes. "Okay. I'll be serious. It's very simple really. You sure you want to know?"

"Tell me already!" She squealed and gave him a mock look of frustration.

"A very long time ago there was this man who impacted everyone who met him because he genuinely cared about each and every person. He would do anything for anyone who needed help or just a kind word. He fed the hungry, healed the sick, and comforted those who suffered inside. He was friendly with the people that everyone else was repulsed by and would have nothing to do with. He was so kind and so compassionate without exception that word spread all over. People came from everywhere just to be close to him and hear him speak about how to love each other and treat each other. Basically, how to live a life that would be fulfilling for all the right reasons. Not because you got something tangible for it but because the more you experienced love and practiced being kind the more you found that love and kindness return to you. Because it was the right thing to do. Because it was good." Jack paused.

"That's obviously not you or you wouldn't be on a bus to Salt Lake." She laughed. "But you care about people because you admire this man?" Hailey asked.

"I definitely admire him." Jack told her. "So much so that I want to be just like him. Well as much like him as I can be. I fall short every single day, but the more I strive to be like him the more I feel my heart grow and the more joy I experience. And I find that it all comes back to me and then some."

"Alright then. Who is he? Some famous humanitarian?" She raised her eyebrows.

Jack grinned. "You could say that. But much of what he taught was controversial and enraged the powers that be so much they conspired and had him executed."

She sat up straight, her eyes wide in disbelief. "What?!" She asked. "Are you kidding me? Who does that?"

"These were powerful men and they were terrified, Hailey." Jack explained. "This man, this teacher was becoming more and more popular and they were losing their control over the people. They ruled by fear and very strict laws and kept their thumb on the people. This man was teaching things that threatened their ability to control the population. People wanted to follow him, wanted him to be their leader instead of these other men. When the people realized that what the men in power were telling them was in direct opposition with what this man taught, he became a threat." He sat back and sighed. "So, they decided he had to be eliminated to protect their positions and power."

"Scandalous." She said, gritting her teeth. "Love is better than power or fame or money."

"I agree and so does he." Jack said.

"He does? So, he's still alive? I thought you said he was executed." She was puzzled.

"Oh, he was." Jack grinned. "But he came back. He's very much alive." He watched her expectantly.

Hailey's eyes grew big then she narrowed them at Jack. "You're messing with me now. What is this, a movie or a book?"

"Both but also it really happened." Jack said leaning in closer. "Do you want me to tell you the whole story from the beginning?"

"Yes!" She said immediately and slapped his arm. "Tell me everything and don't leave out a single detail!"

Jack's heart leapt inside his chest. He started from the beginning and he told her about how the God that made absolutely everything in the universe came to live among us and how he changed everything forever when he did. During the hours to follow she sat wide-eyed, soaking in every detail. She asked questions and commented randomly. She was horrified one moment and giddy the next. She could see all the people Jack told her about in her mind and they were alive and breathing. They became real to her as he described them. Jack had very effectively taken her by the hand and showed her another time and place. By the end of the story she was sobbing. And by the time the bus rolled into Salt Lake, a new soul belonged to Christ and heaven rejoiced.

Jack and Hailey said their goodbyes as they waited for their respective taxis. Hailey hugged Jack and thanked him for caring enough to share the most important thing she had ever been told in her life. He responded in typical Jack style, that it was an honor to have done so. She waved goodbye then took a taxi to a hotel near Brayden's area of the city. Jack chose a hotel relatively close to the bus and train stations. He was not yet sure how much time he would spend in Salt Lake City.

Once he was checked into his hotel room, he pulled out the atlas and began looking for the next place of interest. He decided after Salt Lake he would travel to Green River, a small town with a population of less than 1500. There were canyons and hiking trails nearby which he thought would be fun to explore. After all, the point was to see the country not the inside of hotel rooms.

Jack's stomach rumbled reminding him he had not eaten any real food that day. Protein bars and chips were fine for getting through a bus ride but his body was now demanding a decent meal. He grabbed his cell phone and pulled up a list of restaurants near him. He settled on a Brazilian restaurant that was within walking distance of the hotel.

Hailey had quite an impact on him. Her youth and naiveté were a gift as well as a curse. He thought about his own youth and the crazy notions he had about the way his life was going to be. When he was 7 years old he was going to be a firefighter in New York City. When he was 10 years old he was going to be a weatherman. When he was 12 he was going to be a recording artist. When he was 15 he was going to be a surgeon. It turned out he did go into the medical field but in a slightly different role. He decided on Biomedical Engineering at the end of his junior year of high school and never looked back. Now he had his Masters in the field and an exciting job waiting for him in a city that he had loved from the first moment he visited Uncle Phillip there 14 years ago. He recalled spending time in Boston proper but primarily in the small seaside town called Winthrop where his uncle actually lived. That vacation had sparked in Jack a love of the history and culture of the area. He was excited about starting a new life there. Jack left the restaurant feeling full and content. He got back to his hotel room and watched a movie before going to sleep.

Tuesday morning Jack jotted down places of interest around the city as he enjoyed breakfast at a coffee shop near the hotel. It was surprising how much came up when he started searching out things to do in SLC. He decided to spread his choices over two days, just so he could take his time.

Satisfied that he had a game plan, he finished his breakfast and went back to his hotel to change into shorts, a tee shirt and sneakers. The weather was perfect so he spent the entire day outdoors, returning to his hotel by 9:30 pm. He was in bed by midnight and dreamed about flowers – a vast garden filled with red roses with no end in sight. When the alarm sounded the next morning, he could have sworn he could smell roses in his room.

Chapter Ten

Monday morning Taylor went into the office and told his partner about his vacation plans. Then it was all about tying up loose ends and getting Greg caught up on his accounts. Once he felt like everything had been addressed, he decided to visit the bank. He had substantial savings in addition to his checking account. He made a large withdrawal from his savings account and notified the bank that he would be using his debit card in many different states for an undetermined period of time starting this week. They made a note on the account so unusual spending habits would not trigger fraud alert. Satisfied that he was prepared to travel, he wrapped up his banking and went home.

He packed and tucked his luggage away by the door then he went back in and sat on the bed. Looking around the room he thought about the different places he would be sleeping. None would be as comfortable as this room, the room he had shared with Karen. He glanced over at the picture on the bedside table and felt that familiar ache. He still missed her terribly. Their wedding photo was one of three in the tri-fold frame next to the bed. There they were in the center frame on their wedding day, young and happy. She was breathtaking. Her dark blonde hair was pinned back with soft ringlets framing her lovely face. She was 18 years old on their wedding day. Looking back, he realized they were just children. He gazed at the picture and into those pretty blue eyes of hers and was transported back to that time – the best of times. But no, not really. The best of times came later. He looked to the frame on the left and smiled down at baby Brian's chubby, happy face. His mother was holding him and Taylor was behind her leaning over her shoulder. Both of them were gazing down at the boy. That photograph said it all. From the time he arrived, they were mesmerized by him. The world revolved around Brian. And why not? He was a great kid. He would have been a great man. Taylor felt a lump form in his throat and tears began to sting his eyes. He looked over to the picture on the far right at a much older Brian. This was taken in his last year of life. He lived to be 20 years old. The tears overflowed and spilled down Taylor's cheeks and he sobbed aloud. He folded the frame and carried it to where his bags were sitting. Karen and Brian were going with him on this journey he decided. It was good to have a visual reminder of the family and love he once had. He tucked the frame away in the smaller suitcase. That reminded him of one more thing he definitely needed to take with him. He went into the living room and picked his Bible up from the coffee table. "You may be the most important thing I bring." He said, patting the cover before packing it away as well.

He ordered in some Chinese food and changed into his pajamas after he ate. Then he turned on the television and got caught up on the world news. An earthquake in Asia had killed thousands and spawned a tsunami which killed thousands more. Tension between Israel and the rest of the Middle East was escalating and there were concerns that if attacked, Israel would launch a nuke. Finally, terrorist factions had unleashed tactical assaults throughout Europe and Russia. The correlation to end times prophecy wasn't lost on Taylor. It was a dark time and would undoubtedly get darker. When he had about all he could take of bad news, he turned over to a movie channel. He fell asleep on the couch and woke up around 2:00 am with a terrible thirst. He shuffled into the kitchen and got a glass of water and headed to the bedroom. The lamp beside the bed was dimly lit revealing a body shaped depression on the comforter. It looked as if someone were lying there but only the impression made by their body could be seen, not an actual body. He could hear the rise and fall of breathing and his skin broke out in goosebumps. Slowly whatever was making that depression began to materialize right in front of him. It was Karen and she looked like she did years before Brian died – when she was still happy. She opened her eyes and reached for Taylor.

"Come to bed, honey." She said sleepily. Taylor was rooted to the floor. She sat up. "Stay here with me, Taylor. Don't go anywhere." She smiled and patted his side of the bed. Tempting offer but Taylor still could not move from where he stood. He reached up and touched his face. He seemed to be awake but this couldn't be happening so he must be dreaming.

"I can't stay, Karen. God told me what He wants me to do and I agreed to do it." Taylor explained. He didn't like the way she frowned at him.

"Stay with me instead. We can start over. Don't you want another chance?" Karen was trying her best to convince him to give in and stay. He felt part of him pulling towards her. Of course, he wanted another chance. Who doesn't wish for another chance to be with their loved ones after they are gone? She *was* gone, wasn't she? Yes. She'd been gone for 5 years now. *She died right here in this room*, he thought.

"I'm back and I will stay with you if you just forget this nonsense about God." The sweetness had left her voice and she was beginning to sound annoyed.

"Nonsense about God?" Taylor repeated, narrowing his eyes. "Nothing about God is nonsense. You of all people know better than to suggest such a thing to me, Karen." He didn't like where this dream was headed.

"It *is* nonsense, Taylor." Her face was twisted with anger now. "Why would you listen to a God who murdered our son?" She hissed.

"That was how *you* felt, Karen." He pointed his finger accusingly at her. "But if you recall, I never saw it that way. And you hated me for it. You couldn't stand that fact that I refused to stand by your side and rage against a God who could allow our son to be killed. You resented me for having the faith to believe that God must know more about all of it than we did and that we had no right to question His will." His hand was shaking now. Everything from that terrible time came rushing back. After Brian was killed she started to self-medicate with liquor and pills. It was a combination of these that caused her death. Maybe it was an accident and maybe it wasn't.

"You buried your head in the sand with that 'God's will' garbage, Taylor!" Karen shrieked at him from the bed. She was up on her knees now, shaking her fist at him. "You traded our son for God and you left me behind to drown in the pain by myself."

"That was your choice, Karen." He found he could move now so he walked over to the bed and sat on the edge. "I tried to comfort you but you wouldn't be comforted. I prayed for you and you cursed me. I loved you and took care of you up until the end and you refused to let go of your rage." Taylor reached out and touched her arm. She was cold like stone. "I never gave up on you, Karen. You gave up on me."

"So let me make it up to you then." Her voice softened and she went back to her relaxed posture. She slipped the thin strap of her nightgown down until it fell away from her shoulder. Her eyes blazed with desire and in an instant Taylor understood that this was not a dream. He knew exactly what it was and then he felt it. The room was filled with the oppressive presence of evil. He jumped up from the bed, stumbled backwards and pointed at her with a trembling hand.

"I know who you are! Get away from me! Now!" He yelled. All at once her face morphed from Karen's face to that of a beautiful blonde with full, inviting lips. Her green eyes flashed at him defiantly.

"Okay." She pouted. "For now." She blew him a kiss then vanished.

Taylor found himself back on the couch with the TV playing some horror flick. He got up and ran to the bedroom. It was dark – no lamp was on. He flipped the light switch on which revealed a comforter that was perfectly smooth and a bed that was completely empty. He was suddenly aware that he was drenched in sweat. What an intense dream, if it had been a dream. Who was he trying to fool? He knew it wasn't a dream. God said that Satan would try to discourage him and apparently this was attempt number one. Unfortunately, Taylor felt certain this was only the first of many.

He looked at the clock, which showed 2:12 am. He peeled off his pajamas, took a shower then crawled into bed in just a pair of boxers. He slept soundly until his alarm went off at 7:00 am.

Chapter Eleven

Mary gathered her team together in an empty warehouse in Maryland. It was owned by one of her many corporations that existed only on paper. There was no chance of being interrupted or discovered. The men were hand-picked by Mary for the purpose of doing the preliminary work as they proceeded to contain the Taylor Stratton situation. Each would receive his assignment and was expected to execute it without fail. Known to each other only by last name, part of their contract with Mary required them to disclose very little about themselves. They began to arrive shortly before their scheduled meeting time at 7:30 am.

The first to show up was Finnick – known as Finn, followed by Berk, Taro and finally Sullivan who went by Sully. Mary had done extensive background checks on them before hiring them years ago. They had been utilized before but not for anything this important. It was a gamble on her part and she knew it. The crew sat on metal folding chairs scattered about the break area. The place was filthy. Sully tried his best to dust off his chair before sitting down. Mary stared at him as he fussed over the layer of dirt, trying to get rid of it by blowing at first then by tipping the chair and patting the seat from the other side. Finally he used his hand to wipe it down but then stood looking at his hand unsure what to do about the thick film of grime that now covered his palm.

"Sit." Mary directed him with a pointed finger. He obeyed, still holding out his hand. "What? Didn't Mommy give you a wet-nap before she dropped you off today?" Mary asked condescendingly. He looked at her blankly. No point forging ahead until the distraction was removed. She walked over to the counter where a shop rag was wadded up next to some tools. "Here." She handed it to Sully. He grinned and wiped the dirt from his hand only to discover he had swapped the dirt for grease from the rag. Mary rolled her eyes when she saw him pouting. Could this be an omen? She wondered momentarily then decided it didn't matter. She had to work with what she had. She retrieved the files from the briefcase on the table behind her and handed one to each of the team members.

"Get yourselves familiar with the subjects in these files." She told them as they began thumbing through the documents. "Depending on who I assign for which task, you may be following one or more of these subjects."

Taro spoke up. "When do we kill them?" He asked.

"You don't." Mary sighed. "I will match you to a particular mission and you will receive all the details concerning your directives at that time. Until you are contacted personally concerning YOUR involvement, you need not worry about any long-term plans."

"But we get paid, right?" Sully asked, holding the shop rag by one corner.

"Yes." Mary answered. "And your expenses will be covered."

"How will you contact us?" Berk asked.

"I will call you on your cell just as I did when I arranged this meeting." Mary told him. She felt like she was teaching a kindergarten class. "Any other questions?" They shook their heads. "Good. I assume you are all literate so I will let you read through the mission directives and hold your questions until I return in 30 minutes. I expect you to have read it thoroughly in that time." She grabbed her briefcase and walked out of the warehouse. Thirty minutes later she returned and they were ready for her with plenty of questions. She explained everything in as simplistic terms as she could until they seemed satisfied. The only one she didn't hear from was Finn who didn't comment or ask any questions. He seemed to have a better grasp on the situation than the others. She recalled his background information. He was ambitious and dauntless. He might be her ace in the hole if the others turned out to be duds. She dismissed them and everyone scattered to go about their business and wait for further instructions.

As she drove back to D.C. she thought about her interaction with Taylor in the early hours of the morning. She struck a nerve when she used his dead wife to assess his weaknesses. His most vulnerable areas were his dead son and wife so why not exploit that? She had not been prepared for him catching on so quickly. He was smarter and had more self-control than the average human male. Still she had to admit she had enjoyed dipping her toe in that pool. A worthy opponent was not something she encountered every day. Tricking Taylor was not going to work, that much was evident so more subversive means would be required. She smiled to herself as she played with different ideas for derailing Taylor from this mission he was so committed to. It needed to be subtle so it would fly under his radar. Anything too big would bring divine intervention and that was the last thing she wanted. There were so many ways for her to impede Taylor's progress. And it wasn't just him, there were the other two as well – Jack and Kate. Were they on the move yet?

She called Sully. "I want you on one of the subjects right away. I'll text you the current location shortly and you are to follow and watch for opportunities to detain. Do not screw this up, Sully." She hung up and called her source for the subject's location and texted Sully the information. She continued towards D.C., where she would update Cassian. Then she would get Taylor's location and watch for opportunities for sabotage.

Chapter Twelve

It was a beautiful day and Taylor was anxious to get moving. He called his brother. "The place is all yours. I put clean sheets on the bed for you but when you do a load of laundry, could you wash the sheets and the pajamas that are in the hamper?" Matt said he would and wished his brother a safe and happy vacation. Taylor paused, wondering if he would be around to speak to Matt again or not. "Thanks again for helping me out. I love you, little brother."

Taylor loaded his luggage into the Maxima, then made one last pass to make sure everything was set before locking up the house. He sat parked in the driveway for a few minutes, looking at his home. He smiled as he felt himself let go of all he had in the world. Everything was about to change. He wasn't going to be the same person when he returned – *if* he returned. The realization hit him that he was doing in the literal sense exactly what Christ had said was required for His disciples. Leave your home, your family, and your possessions and follow Him. And for a man who was choosing to lose everything, he felt like he was gaining everything. Taylor saluted, then put the car in reverse and left his life behind.

He hit a little bit of commuter traffic on his way out of town but it eased off after 9:30. He drove north on I-15 for several hours until it was time to stop and eat. He pulled over at a gas station to fill up and then drove a little further until he found a place to eat. As he waited for his meal, he pulled up a map of I-15 and wondered where he was going to be this time tomorrow. He had not received any urges or inclinations to make radical direction changes or get off the I-15. He felt at peace with the road and the direction so far.

This "rose" business was a mystery. He kept thinking about this girl or woman he was supposed to find and… and what? He didn't have a clue. *That's the beauty of faith*, he thought. You just don't worry about what comes next. The answers are revealed in God's time, not man's time. That made him smile because he wasn't always so accepting and patient. Taylor had once been an impatient man, arrogant, full of pride and he thought everything should happen according to his wants and needs. And when it didn't work out that way, he became angry. He looked back on that time now and it made him cringe. It wasn't good to dwell on past sins but sometimes it was a valuable measuring stick to remind a person how far they had come. But he didn't get this far by himself. It was all God's doing. Taylor alone was an inept fool who, if given a 50/50 chance would choose wrong 99% of the time. Years of doing it his way and falling flat on his face had taught him that he really did not know what was best for his life. It was when he came to that realization and handed God control of his life that everything changed for the better. Being young and foolish is hard enough. Being young and foolish and having no moral compass, no guiding light – well, that was disaster.

That's where he was when he met Karen. Memories of her were tormenting and bittersweet. There had been so much love and joy but that had turned into hatred and resentment on her part. From the dark into the light then back into the dark again, so goes the merry-go-round of life. But no more, Taylor resolved. He had fought his way out of the darkness and he knew what it was like to feel the warmth of the sun on his face. He would stay in the light where God could see him and he could see God – well, metaphorically speaking of course.

It was almost 2:00 pm when he got back on the road after lunch. He drove with the windows down and the music loud, listening to a Contemporary Christian Music station on satellite radio. It brought a wave of nostalgia and memories of singing and playing air guitar and air drums with Brian in the car as they drove with "Jesus Freak" cranked as loud as his stereo would go. He had so many happy memories of Brian. How he longed to share everything that was happening right now with his son. Brian was the one person who would have understood and embraced all this. He missed his buddy but he refused to feel sorry for himself. All things serve God's purpose and it was not up to him to understand or agree with how God runs his business. He might have thought he was important enough to be kept in the loop when he was young but not anymore. Was losing Brian part of God's plan to perfect acceptance and faith? Regardless, he didn't feel bad for his son. Brian was in paradise just waiting for Taylor to finish up down here and join him. He could almost see his son's face with that notorious expression that said, "Okay, get on with it already!" That made Taylor laugh out loud. "I'm doing my best, boy. Keep your shorts on." He said to the empty passenger seat.

By 9:00 pm he was ready to stop for the night. He drove until he saw highway signs indicating hotels ahead. He pulled off I-15 and found a decent place to stay. He was just south of Las Vegas and didn't want to deal with that place other than breezing right passed it in the morning. He checked in and the clerk gave him a key to a room on the first floor. After a shower and some food, he turned in for the night and dreamed of a meadow of roses as far as the eye could see and woke up refreshed the next morning, ready to see what was next.

Chapter Thirteen

His second day in SLC Jack visited Peace Gardens and then went on to Memory Grove, which was a botanical garden with hiking trails, veteran memorials and a replica of the Liberty Bell. It was late afternoon when he finally took a break in a busy area of the park. He was sitting on a bench munching on a protein bar when he saw a little boy about four years old have a total meltdown, mere feet away from him. The boy was crying and screaming for his mommy. Jack didn't see anyone nearby responding to the child. He had a growing sense of dread that this kid would be easy prey for any shady character who might snatch him up under the guise of taking him to his mother. He was standing very close to Jack when their eyes met. Jack smiled at the boy.

"Hey, little man." He said to the boy. "It's going to be okay. If you wait where you are, your mommy will find you very soon." The little boy stopped crying.

"She will?" The boy sniffled and wiped his nose with the back of his hand.

"Sure! I'll bet she's on her way back here right now." Jack looked around hoping to see a woman running towards them but there were just people meandering around taking pictures and videos and such. "Why don't we play a game while we wait for her?"

"Okay!" The boy said and climbed up on the bench next to Jack.

Jack thought for a moment and asked, "Do you know your ABC's?"

"Yes!" The boy had already forgotten about being lost.

85

"Great! Let's take turns with the letters. I'll say one and you say the letter that comes next."

"A!" The boy laughed.

"B!" Jack said, acting like he had to think about it for a second.

"C!" The boy shouted joyfully, kicking his legs up and down.

"Umm. Hmm, let me see… what is next?" Jack rubbed his chin and squinted his eyes like he was concentrating really hard. Meanwhile he was scanning the park for the child's mom, hopeful she would show up before they got to Z. "Can you give me a clue?"

"It's D!" The boy giggled.

"Hey, you're really smart. What is your name anyway?" Jack was stalling.

"Efan Josuf Wicharson!" The boy told him. Translation: Ethan Joseph Richardson. Cute kid.

"Well I'm Jack, Ethan. I am pleased to meet you!" He shook the boy's small hand. "Do you know what letter Ethan starts with?

"E!" Ethan squealed and pumped his legs up and down again.

Jack looked around again. No mom but lots of tourists, photographers and a girl sitting nearby obviously taking video on her cell phone. No one who looked predatory thank God.

"You are right. High five!" Jack held his palm up and Ethan slapped it with great vigor. Jack pretended to be hurt. "Wow! You are really strong! That hurt!" He shook his hand and pretended to be in pain. Ethan looked concerned until Jack winked at him.

"You're not hurt! You're a playin'!" Ethan laughed. Jack liked this kid. He was sharp.

"Okay, you got me. But you are really strong. How old are you? Forty? Forty-five?" Jack asked.

Ethan giggled again. "Noooooo! I'm this many!" He used his left hand to help put his right pinky down so only his thumb and the first three fingers were up.

"Four? Are you sure about that? You're awful strong for being this many." And Jack did the same thing with his fingers as Ethan had. The boy nodded his head adamantly.

"How many are you, Jack?" Ethan asked.

Jack held up all ten fingers and said, "This many!" and he flashed his hands open and closed a dozen times. Ethan laughed so hard he had to hold his tummy. The sound of his laughter made Jack happy. What a great kid. But where was his mother?

"You're too many!" Ethan said finally. "I can't count that big yet. I can count to 10 though." He waited for Jack to call him on it so he could prove he could really do it.

"Really?" Jack acted surprised. "I don't know if I can even count that many!"

"Yes, you can!" Ethan reached out and playfully smacked Jack on the leg. "You want me to show you?"

"I sure do!" Jack told him.

Ethan started counting and before he got to the number seven a woman came running up red faced and frantic.

"ETHAN JOSEPH!!!!" She was screaming.

Ethan stopped counting. "Uh oh." He whispered.

As she approached her focus shifted from the boy to the man sitting next to her son.

"What are you doing with my son?" She bellowed.

"We're counting to ten!" Ethan answered.

"Hush!" His mother said, grabbing her young son by the arm and yanking him off the bench. "Did this man try to take you?" She demanded. The boy nodded his head.

Jack's heart stopped. No! That wasn't right. The woman lost her mind right then and there and started screaming.

"Help! Help! This man tried to take my son!"

Ironically a security guard was already there. He had shown up right as the mother came running up to them earlier. "What's the problem here?" He wanted to know, narrowing his eyes at Jack. He was a young man, average height and slim build with rather shaggy sandy brown hair. His brown eyes were set close and he had a beak-like nose. His mouth was set in a perpetual smirk.

"He was trying to kidnap my son!" Ethan's mother wailed.

"Is that right?" The security guard knelt down to Ethan's level. The boy nodded. Jack was sure the boy didn't understand what was being asked of him. This was turning very bad very fast.

"I assure you I was not trying to abduct the child." Jack started to explain. "He was crying for his mother and I simply started talking to him to calm him down until his mom found him. I knew if he stayed in one place she'd eventually make her way back here." The woman glared at him and the security guard gave him a suspicious look.

"Sir, I need you to turn around please. "The security guard was pulling out zip ties. Jack couldn't believe what was happening.

"Sir? Officer?" Jack looked for a name tag.

"Sullivan." The security guard answered as he slid the zip tie cuffs onto Jack's wrists.

"Officer Sullivan." Jack turned back around and spoke in a calm tone. "You seem like a reasonable man. I was simply sitting on this bench making sure the boy was safe until his mother returned. In no way was I trying to take the child."

"He's telling the truth." A young man approached. "And that girl has the whole thing on video on her phone." He pointed to the young woman who had been sitting close to them the whole time but had moved off as soon as the mother came into the picture. Mom was making too much noise and ruining the video that the girl was shooting of her unsuspecting boyfriend and the girl he was cheating on her with.

Sullivan looked both surprised and extremely annoyed by the witness who had stepped forward. The stranger was a young man in his late teens, early twenties. He was slim with long blond hair and a very handsome face.

"My name is Jordan. You will want to put that in the report you give to your superiors." The young man said leaning in, his blue eyes drilling Sullivan's, making him recoil. Some kind of unspoken conversation seemed to pass between them and Jack was suddenly very curious about these two. It was almost felt like they knew each other and had a long-standing grudge.

"Okay, *Jordan*." Sullivan said. "What did you see and or hear?" He wasn't even trying to disguise the look of contempt on his face.

"So glad you asked, *Sully*." Jordan returned the attitude. The security guard winced noticeably and touched his hand to his stomach. Jordan nodded and continued. "I was right over here and I witnessed the entire thing. The boy was screaming bloody murder because his mother had lost him." Jordan turned his attention to the mother. "Perhaps when you talk to your lover on your cell phone you should try not to get so distracted that you completely forget that you have a four-year old boy with you." The woman stepped back and looked like she had just been slapped in the face.

Oh Snap! Jack thought. Clearly, that had struck a nerve.

Jordan went on. "This man was actually calming the boy down and telling him to stay put so his mom would find him in a few minutes. Of course, it took longer than a few minutes because she was engrossed in scheming how she would slip out of her house later tonight and meet up with her lover without her husband becoming suspicious." He paused, glaring at the woman who now looked like all the blood had drained from her face. She was speechless. Jordan continued. "This nice man distracted Ethan who was scared out of his mind…" Another disapproving look to the mother. "…by playing games like taking turns saying their ABC's and counting. All while sitting on a bench in clear view of everyone here." He turned his attention from the mother to Sullivan. "So, Sully, tell me how that translates into he's kidnapping the child and you are somehow justified in cuffing him?"

"She said!" Sully pointed to the mother.

"Well, I thought…" She stopped abruptly and rethought her statement. "Ethan said yes when I asked him if the man was trying to take him!"

Jordan gave her a look of pity. "Ethan, did this man take you to Mars?" He asked the boy. Ethan nodded. "Did he take clowns and elephants there too?" Ethan nodded. Jordan looked up at the mother then at Sully. "I think you get the point." They both looked down at the ground.

"Okay Ethan, I want you to remember when you were crying, okay?" Ethan nodded. "Did he ever ask you to leave with him?" Ethan shook his head. "Is that a yes or a no?"

"No." Ethan said. "He said to wait for Mommy."

"Did he touch you?" Jordan asked the boy.

"He high fived me a cause I know Efan starts with E!" Ethan said.

"That's it?" Jordan asked. Ethan nodded again, smiling. The girl with the video looked over and Jordan flagged her down. "Hey, come here, will you?" She walked over.

"You were here the whole time taking video." Jordan said and she nodded. "You pick up sound on there right?" He asked pointing at the phone.

"Sure." She said.

"Can you play your video for Mrs. Richardson here and Sully?" Jordan asked. She agreed and played the recording from the beginning as everyone moved in close to listen. She cranked the volume all the way up. As expected, for a while all you could hear was background noise because there was no talking, only visual. Then the boy started crying and Jack and Ethan's entire audio conversation followed exactly as Jack and Jordan said it took place. When it was over Sully looked enraged but he cut the zip tie cuffs off Jack and mumbled an apology. The mother was embarrassed but she also apologized.

Jack heard Jordan say to Sully, "Nice try. Better luck next time." Jack wasn't sure what that meant and wasn't sure he wanted to know. "By the way, how are those abs of yours?" Jordan asked.

Sully grimaced. His reply was peppered with obscenities spoken under his breath. Jordan stood tall, puffing his chest out and started moving towards Sully who quickly backed down and retreated. Both men were young and not terribly big but both gave the impression that there was more than meets the eye between them. Jordan had a commanding presence that Jack couldn't quite explain.

"Bye Jack!" Ethan yelled happily as he ran to Jack with his hand up to high five him again. Jack again pretended to be hurt and Ethan giggled.

"Bye Ethan. You be good for your mommy, okay? You only get one and mommies are very special." Jack told Ethan. Mrs. Richardson looked even more ashamed but mouthed the words, "thank you," to Jack.

Ethan and his mother left and Jack stood there looking at Jordan. He started to speak, to thank him for what he did but Jordan held up his hand.

"No need." Jordan said. "You were being set up."

"What?" Jack was shocked. "I don't know any of those people. Why would they…?"

"I know." Jordan put his hand on Jack's shoulder and Jack felt a tingle like a mild electric shock when he did. "Unfortunately, they know *you*." Jordan gave him a friendly pat. He started to walk away and then turned back around. "This is just the beginning so be careful, Jack." He advised and then he walked away. Jack simply watched in stunned silence as the young man left.

Jack had never been so happy to end a day in his entire life. He went over and over the event in his head and dissected every nuance and detail. Considering what Jordan had told him about being set up, he could now make sense of the arrival of the security guard at the precise moment Ethan's mother started making accusations. Also, the fact that Sully was so eager to cuff Jack and haul him away was more plausible if it were planned in advance. The level of anger displayed was out of proportion as well – unless it was a setup and Sully was really out to get him.

But why? Jack was a tourist traveling through the area with no ties to anyone. Why would anyone want to set him up and detain him? For what purpose? The other big puzzle was Jordan. Jack had surveyed the area and saw everyone who was around when he was looking for the mother. He simply could not recall seeing Jordan at the park at any time that day. Much like Sully, Jordan seemed to have materialized out of thin air at just the right time. Come to think of it, if Jordan hadn't shown up Jack would probably be sitting in jail right now instead of lying on the bed in his hotel room. He was indebted to the young man who came forward as a witness, but the Jordan and Sully dynamic seemed more like an old and festering grievance rather than two strangers with opposing roles in a conflict. Finally, the warning from Jordan that this was just the beginning made Jack wonder what he had missed. For some reason, the idea gave him the weebies, like he had one foot in another realm and one in this world. He decided then and there that his time in Salt Lake City had come to an end and he would be moving on in the morning. He skipped dinner and went to bed early, afraid to leave his room for fear of another encounter like the one earlier that day.

CHAPTER 14

By 9:00 am Taylor was out the door and in the car to search out a good place for breakfast. His trusty "Restaurant Finder" app on his phone had directed him several miles west of the hotel to a mom and pop café that served a home style breakfast buffet that would easily feed an army. The food was great, service was excellent, and the staff was friendly. He left the café and headed back to the hotel where he relaxed until it got closer to checkout time at 11:00. At 10:50 he put his suitcase in the trunk and got into the car to drive around to the front of the hotel and check out. He pressed on the brake and pushed the start button. Nothing. He looked at the dash for any warning lights and saw nothing. He repeated the process which he'd done hundreds of times with this car and still nothing, not even a click. Maybe the battery was dead. He pressed the trunk button and the lid sprung up. That wouldn't happen with a dead battery, would it? Then he opened the door and saw the dome lights came on, so it definitely was not the battery. He went around, retrieved his suitcase from the trunk and went back into his room. He called the front desk and told them he might not be checking out after all and to put him down tentatively for another night. Then he looked on the internet for an auto mechanic nearby. There was a shop about 10 miles east of the hotel. Next, he called AAA and told them he needed a tow and gave them the address. He went back out and emptied all his belongings from the Maxima and took them into his room for safe keeping.

The tow truck arrived about an hour later and Taylor was riding shotgun on the way to the garage chatting with the driver along the way. The driver's name was Weldon. He had a wife, Sarah and newborn son named Caleb. He told Taylor how he and Sarah weren't getting much sleep since the little one arrived. The dark circles and puffiness under his eyes were validation enough of that claim. Taylor recalled how it had been with Brian and assured Weldon that it was tough but it would get better. He told the driver the story about Brian projectile vomiting all over his mother-in-law who was dressed to the nines for Easter Sunday service.

"And because she refused to be late or miss service she had to change clothes at our house. There wasn't time for her to go home." Taylor remembered the event vividly and recalled how hard it was for him not to laugh that day. His mother-in-law was fuming. "She was a rather large woman and my wife was very slim so she couldn't wear anything of Karen's. She ended up having to squeeze into a pair of Karen's maternity pants and a top. The pants were way too short so she was flooding big time. The maternity clothes back then weren't nearly as stylish as they are now, Weldon. They were very obviously maternity clothes. So here comes Jane marching into Easter Sunday service wearing a pair of black maternity pants 3 inches too short, a pair of silver flip flops and a neon pink maternity tee shirt that had "Almost Done" written across the chest with an arrow pointing down to the belly where a huge oven spanned the area where the baby bump would be sticking out. In her case it was just too many jelly donuts." Weldon was laughing so hard he was having trouble seeing the road. Taylor continued. "Now mind you, this was a big day when all the ladies dressed up in the best of the best in their wardrobe. Everywhere you looked were women in hats and pearls and fancy dresses with designer heels and matching purses. These were the women that Jane always looked at judgmentally on a regular Sunday when she thought they weren't put together as well as she was. That day she got taken down a peg or two. Pride is a terrible thing, Weldon. Watching the proud fall flat on their faces is truly a humbling experience. But I won't lie. I did enjoy every minute of it!"

Weldon pulled the truck into the parking lot of Monk's Automotive Service just as Taylor finished his story. They got out and Taylor went inside to speak to the mechanic while Weldon unhooked the Maxima. The mechanic's name was Ronnie and he was around Taylor's age which made him feel pretty good. He had feared getting someone fresh out of high school who might not know what he was doing. Taylor explained the problems he had experienced that morning and his observations. Ronnie took the smart key and wrote down all Taylor's information, including his cell phone number. He promised to look things over and call Taylor when he found out what needed to be done but it would be later in the day before he could get to it since they were pretty busy with cars that were ahead of his. Taylor said it wasn't a problem, thanked him and they shook hands.

When he turned to walk out of the shop, Taylor noticed Weldon was still hanging around outside so he went out to speak to him.

"Hop in and I'll give you a lift back to your hotel." Weldon offered.

"You sure that's not out of your way, Weldon?" Taylor didn't want to be an imposition.

"Nope. Gotta go right by there on my way back anyways." He assured him.

"Well okay then. Thanks, man!" Taylor climbed into the tow truck and they headed back, exchanging humorous stories on the way. Weldon told Taylor about the time he was called out on a tow job for a group of drunk girls who broke down on their way back from Vegas. Four of them were crammed into the cab of his truck and were as rowdy and out of control as can be except for the girl who was the designated driver and she was clearly disgusted by her other friends' behavior. One was throwing up in her purse. Another was obsessed with the hair on her toes and kept pulling her own leg up so she could get her foot as close to her face as possible as well as the faces of the other girls. Another was in tears because her boyfriend refused to answer her phone calls. She kept calling and leaving messages one after another for the entire ride which was over an hour.

"That was the longest hour of my life, Taylor." He chuckled. "But when my son was born I was thanking my lucky stars all day for having a boy instead of a girl. No way was I ready to deal with any of that later on in my life!"

"Boys are easy." Taylor told him. "Caleb will be your best buddy."

"Yeah, I think he will be." Weldon smiled as he pulled into the hotel parking lot. "Home sweet home, my friend." He said as they came to a stop.

"Hey thanks, Weldon." While they were driving Taylor had discreetly palmed three one-hundred-dollar bills. He slipped the neatly folded bills to Weldon when they shook hands. "Take your bride out for a nice dinner." He said clapping Weldon on the arm with his other hand.

Weldon stared at the cash in his hand. "No sir! You're paid up already through AAA. I can't accept this." He protested.

"Sure, you can." Taylor said and climbed out. "You blessed me with your company and even gave me a ride back here. It's my privilege to bless you in return." He shut the door and waved. He watched as Weldon unfolded the bills and saw that it was more than just a single $100 bill. He looked up with tears filling his eyes and smiled at Taylor and shook his head as if in disbelief. He threw the truck into gear, waved and drove away.

A small voice inside Taylor's head whispered, "Thank you, God. Now we can buy some groceries." Taylor looked around but he was alone. He realized that was Weldon's voice he heard. *How is that possible?* He thought. *You know.* Came the answer from deep inside his brain. He looked up to the sky, so blue and clear on this beautiful day and gave thanks before going back to his room.

****

Weldon walked through the front door of his house two hours before his wife Sarah would normally be starting dinner, carrying half a dozen plastic bags from the grocery store. Sarah had just put Caleb down for a nap when she heard Weldon come in. She rushed to the living room to greet him and stopped short when she saw her husband grinning ear to ear with grocery bags hanging from his hands.

"What's going on?" She asked with a hint of fear in her voice. She knew there wasn't enough money in their bank account to buy one bag's worth of groceries much less the amount he was holding.

"A lot more of these out in the car." He lifted his arms. "Can you come help?" He winked and walked into the kitchen. She stood rooted to the living room floor.

"Honey, what have you done? We can't –" He came up from behind and lifted her off her feet, cutting her words off before she could finish. He spun her around like you would a child. She giggled and insisted he put her down.

"What is it you always say?" He put her down and took her by the hand and led her out to the car. He showed her the trunk which was FULL of groceries. "God is good, all the time?"

"And all the time, God is good." She finished for him, barely able to speak above a whisper. "Sweet Jesus, thank you. Where did all this come from, Weldon?"

"I just told you." He laughed and planted a kiss on her cheek. "Come on and help me get all this inside. We have a lot of stuff to put away." He started grabbing bags and hurried into the house. Sarah did the same and followed after him.

While they put all the food and household items away, Weldon told his wife about his encounter with Taylor Stratton. By the time he finished she was in tears.

"How could he have known? Are you certain you didn't say anything about us not having any money and the food almost gone?" She coaxed.

"I didn't say a thing or even hint at anything." Weldon swore to her. She gave him that look and he knew what was coming next. It made him smile.

"Okay mister." She said with her hands on her hips. "Is this enough to convince you to come to church with me on Sunday?"

Weldon nodded and pulled his wife close. He kissed her softly. "Yes ma'am. I'd say that's the least I can do for Him after what He just did for us."

"Finally." Sarah squeezed her husband tight then pushed him away. "Oh my gosh! I have so many choices, how will I decide what to make for supper?"

"No cooking for you tonight, my love." Weldon said, pulling cash from his wallet. "We're getting your favorite Chinese food delivered tonight." Sarah started jumping up and down with excitement. Just an hour ago her stomach was in knots because she didn't know what they were going to do. Now she had a kitchen full of food and was being treated to her favorite meal. *God is very good indeed*, she thought.

****

Back in his hotel room, Taylor spent the next hour on his knees in prayer. His mind was reeling with the implications of the events of the day. His car not starting was no accident. Did God orchestrate that or did He just turn something bad into something good for His glory? Was he meant to meet Weldon and help him and his family in some small way all along or did the Lord use that circumstance to bless them all? What other events would come from his broken-down Maxima – a car that never had problems, he might add. Taylor knew it was not a coincidence or a random meaningless occurrence. Something else hinges on the other events of life. Like a malfunctioning alarm clock that kept a man from getting to work on time at one of the World Trade Center Towers on the morning of 9/11.

Taylor said aloud. "Lord I wonder what my delay in travel today will produce. What will I avoid or what will I encounter as a result?" He did not get an answer, which was just fine.

It was almost 4:00 when Ronnie called and said they could not find anything wrong with the car, but it still would not start. He would have to take the smart key over to the Nissan dealership and have them check it out to see if there could be a problem there. He would drop it off on his way home and they should have an answer tomorrow. Taylor thanked him and hung up.

"So, I cool my jets here for another night." He said to the empty room.

That night Taylor dreamed about Brian. His son was about the age he would be now and was riding in the passenger seat of the Maxima talking to Taylor about music, sports and movies. Then Brian asked him a question that surprised him.

"What would you risk for God?" He gave his father a sober look.

"Anything. Everything." Taylor answered. "I picked up and left my job and my home…"

"Yes, but would you risk your life?" Brian narrowed his eyes. "Like stepping in front of a bullet to save someone. That sort of risk."

Anyone would be willing to do that for a loved-one but would he be so quick to give his life for a stranger? "I am not sure how I would react to a situation like that, Brian. Why do you ask?"

Brian's eyes bore into Taylor's relentlessly. "You're going to be faced with that decision. When it comes down to it, will you step up? It doesn't necessarily mean you have to die. The question is, will you be courageous enough to act without fear or hesitation?"

"I hope so." Taylor sighed, feeling out of his depth.

"I hope so too." Brian smiled. "A lot is hanging in the balance."

"Can we go back to talking about baseball, kiddo?" Taylor joked.

Brian laughed. "Next time, Pops." And he vanished before Taylor's eyes.

CHAPTER 15

Cassian summoned Mary to his office where he scolded her for the outcome of the sabotage to Taylor's car.

"Well, we lost another prospect thanks to this roving witness for God. Even without transportation he managed to turn it around and sprinkle his magical do-gooder dust all over a tow truck driver who has now had a change of heart about his spiritual commitments. Nice, Mary." Cassian's face was red.

Mary shrugged. "So what? That's one guy who was on the fence anyway. Calm down already."

"No Mary, I won't calm down. Is this going to be how you operate? Your attempts to accomplish something for us turns into an advantage for *them?*" He asked, teeth clenched.

Mary looked at her nails thinking she needed a manicure soon. The polish was chipping and was starting to look shabby. She stood up and walked over to Cassian and put her finger in his face. "Need I remind you that I have NO control over what God does to turn my efforts into something beneficial for them?" Her voice had that hard edge that gave Cassian pause. "Maybe you should remember who is who in this deal. I can only control so much."

"Well you need to get control over the Jack Anderic situation. Your guy in Salt Lake City dropped the ball in a big way and Jack is on the move again. You were successful in delaying Taylor but your crew is batting zero right now. I suggest you get someone else on Jack and make sure they get the job done this time." Cassian walked over to the window and looked out at the city. "We're done here." He said and waved his hand at her dismissively.

Mary picked up her bag and walked out of the office annoyed by Cass' smug attitude but feeling faultless in her actions. She had successfully delayed Taylor. His car is not working and he is behind schedule which is exactly what she wanted. Subtle and effective. As far as Sully was concerned, she wasn't surprised he had failed but she would address that later. She dialed Berk and told him to prepare to follow Jack when he received a location and look for opportunities to put him on lock down. Berk said he was ready as soon as he got the info on where the subject was. She told him the last attempt by Sully had failed and Berk was expected to succeed. He made a few derogatory remarks about Sully and stated he wasn't surprised he didn't get the job done. Apparently, they didn't get along well. Berk promised he would do better than Sully and hung up.

CHAPTER 16

The day after the incident in the park, Jack was on the Amtrak to Green River which was 180 miles away. The ride took 4 hours and was a step up in comfort from the bus. Once he arrived in Green River he got a cab to a hotel on Main Street. He checked in a little after 7:00 pm.

By 8:00 pm Jack had showered and changed and was hungry. He called the front desk from his room phone.

"Where's a good place to eat around here?" Jack asked the desk clerk.

"Ray's Tavern over on Broadway. It isn't much to look at on the outside but the good food keeps the place pretty busy." The clerk told him. "Go west on main for about 3 miles and make a left on Broadway. You can't miss the place."

"I'll try it out, thanks." Jack told him and hung up. He called a cab to take him to Ray's and was walking up to the tavern less than 10 minutes later. The neon "Ray's" sign and the huge arrow illuminated the night sky. The clerk was right. While this place wasn't fancy it was loaded with character. Before he made it to the door he heard something to his left that concerned him. It was a woman sobbing. Without thinking twice Jack turned and walked in the direction of the sound. In the parking lot almost all the way around back he saw a white pickup truck and a woman sitting on the ground leaning up against the front driver's side tire crying her eyes out. She blew her nose with a tissue and looked up at Jack with a startled look in her eyes.

"I'm sorry, miss." Jack approached her slowly and squatted down to her level. "Do you need help?"

"I locked myself out of my truck and I have to get home before my babysitter leaves my little one there alone." She choked the words out between sobs.

"Do you have a phone?" Jack asked. "Do you need to call someone? Tell me what I can do to help you." The woman's eyes grew wide and she started smiling.

A male voice behind Jack said, "You can give me all your money for starters."

Jack felt something strike his head and he started to fade out but he was only dazed. He felt the hard sole of a boot on his back push him over and hands fumbling in his back pocket to get to his wallet. He watched helplessly as the man crossed in front of him and helped the woman up. Then they climbed into the truck and took off. He rolled over and saw the truck turn right from the parking lot. After a moment, he got himself together and called a cab to take him back to the hotel. Luckily, he had some cash in his front pocket and the man who mugged him didn't bother checking there. The cab showed up and the driver asked Jack if he needed to go to the hospital.

"I'm fine. Just to take me to the hotel." Jack assured him. He was looking out the window on the drive back when he saw the white truck parked at a gas station.

"Pull over!" Jack shouted at the cab driver. "Drive around the side of that station and stop." The cabby did as Jack told him without question. Jack handed him some cash and jumped out. He saw the guy who had jumped him and the girl who had been the decoy standing outside the truck messing with something in the truck bed. He noticed they were much younger than he had thought initially. They weren't much more than kids really. He was going to get his wallet back and hopefully scare them enough that they would think twice about doing something like that again. Brazenly Jack walked up behind the duo.

"Give me my wallet back and I won't press charges." He said to the back of the guy's head. As the man began to turn to face Jack he swung his fist and clocked Jack in the temple. The lights went out completely this time. When Jack came to again sometime later he was sitting on the floor of what appeared to be an abandoned filling station. His wrists were tied behind a pole that was supporting the ceiling. There was enough moonlight that he could see his surroundings. By the look and smell of the place it had been empty for many years and no one came here anymore except kids looking for a place to smoke weed or get into other mischief. He pulled on the rope that bound him to the pole.

"Oh no, Mister! Please don't call the cops on us!" The girl chided from the shadows. The guy with her laughed.

"You can't come into our town and start making demands, you freak!" The guy stepped out of the shadows and kicked Jack in the ribs. "We take what we want and you just go back where you came from. That's how it works."

"I think we need to ditch this loser." The girl suggested.

"I think you may be right. Let's get out of here."

They started to walk away and the girl added, "We should go to The Mill and celebrate." And they disappeared out of sight. Unfortunately, Jack saw them reappear outside the windows with a big red gas can. The man was pouring gasoline all around the perimeter of the building. This wasn't good. Given time Jack could have figured out a way to free himself and get out, but if the building was on fire that was going to give him precious little time to get loose. He watched the guy trail the gasoline away from the building several feet before he lit a match and dropped it, but Jack did not panic. The truck sped away and he stood up inching his bound wrists up the pole as he went. He was looking around for something he might use to free himself when he heard a voice in his head. "Scream for help." It spoke with such authority that Jack started screaming without an argument.

CHAPTER 17

Taylor woke up with the dream about Brian fresh on his mind. He wasn't sure what the day would bring or if he would have his car back at some point but he knew he was hungry. He decided to take a cab back to the mom and pop joint and enjoy that impressive buffet again. As he ate his mind kept returning to the dream. There was a message or a warning there and it had given him a lot to think about. When the time came – when the rubber met the road – what would he do? Would he act without thinking and be heroic or would he freeze like a deer in headlights and get waylaid by whatever was speeding towards him?

It was a little after 1:00 pm when Ronnie called and told Taylor that the smart key had to be reprogrammed. They hadn't seen anything like it at the dealership but it looked as if something had wiped the programming away. They would have it reprogrammed and if the car started and everything checked out, Ronnie would call and he could come get his car. His phone rang at 2:30 with good news about his car. Everything had checked out and it seems it was in fact a problem with the smart key. Taylor called a cab to take him to Monk's where he paid their bill. He was informed that the dealership had a bill for Taylor as well so he called from the garage and gave the receptionist his credit card number to take care of his balance with them. With the financials settled, he got into his car and held his breath. He pressed on the brake and hit the start button. The engine roared to life, as it always had before. He exhaled and smiled. *Welcome back*, he thought. He left Monk's and went back to the hotel where he loaded up his belongings and checked out.

He was on the road again by 3:15. He continued driving north on I-15 into Utah then without giving it any conscious thought he steered the Maxima onto I-70 heading east. It felt natural to make the direction change. He took heed to the signs announcing there would be no services for 100 miles between Salina and Green River and stopped to fill his gas tank. He also took advantage of the opportunity to use the restroom and get water and snacks. Feeling fully prepared for the stretch of desolate highway he got back on I-70 and drove east.

As soon as he crossed into Green River at 9:30 that evening, Taylor felt a heightened awareness. He slowed down and waited for some kind of direction. When he felt a strong urge to turn off the main road he obeyed. He turned off that road as well onto what could only be described as a "back road" which signs indicated was Johnson Bridge Road. He reduced his speed considerably because it was pitch black out there and the road was narrow and winding. The dream he had the night before was suddenly back on his mind. All the hair on his arms and back of his neck was standing straight up. Something was about to happen.

Taylor didn't have to wait long to find out. "Pull off the road now" he was prompted. He immediately turned right where a large driveway entrance appeared beyond the shoulder. The first thing he noticed was flames around the bottom of a small building that appeared to be an old abandoned gas station. The faded FINA sign was leaning hard to the left on a pole that looked like it would come down with the next strong gust of wind.

When Taylor stopped the car he felt prompted to go inside. The voice originating from deep within his mind was forceful and not to be denied. He turned off the headlights and as soon as he opened his car door he heard a man screaming for help from inside

110

the building. Someone was inside and Taylor would have to break a window to get in to reach him. He quickly made his way around to his trunk and grabbed the tire iron. Then he saw the small emergency tool kit lying next to his suitcase and opened it to retrieve a pocket knife. He slid the knife into his front pocket and walked up to the building.

******

From inside the building Jack watched as the faint glow of headlights appeared from the road becoming brighter by the moment. He kept screaming even though he doubted anyone would ever hear him. But as the vehicle approached it slowed down and surprisingly it turned in. The car came to a stop and its headlights blinded him momentarily. He watched as a man got out of the car, took something from his trunk then walked boldly through the flames and shattered the large window in the front of the building. As the man approached Jack stopped yelling.

Taylor walked up to him and said, "I'm here, buddy. You're going to be fine."

"I can't believe you found me! I hope you can find something to cut this rope. My hands are tied." Jack said, his voice hoarse from screaming for who knows how long.

"I've got you covered, brother." Taylor pulled out his pocket knife to cut the ropes that bound Jack to the pole then he grabbed an old fire extinguisher off the wall by what used to be the cash register counter. He knew it was a longshot but figured it was worth a try. Broken glass crunched under his shoes as he walked

111

back to the hole where the front window used to be and triggered the extinguisher. Miraculously it worked. The flames in that one spot were smothered enough for them to get out of the building.

"I have to find the people who tied me up and get my wallet back." Jack rubbed his wrists where the rope had burned his skin.

"I take it you know where to find these people, whoever they are?" Taylor asked as they walked to the car.

"After they tied me up the girl said they should head over to The Mill to celebrate." Jack recalled. His heart was pounding like a jackhammer. He wasn't typically a confrontational person but he had been robbed and left for dead. He was not at peace with letting this go.

Taylor stopped and put his hand on Jack's shoulder. "Maybe we need to get you checked out at a hospital first."

"I'm okay." Jack said, grateful for Taylor's concern. "I think my pride is more injured than my body." He laughed and it pulled at his sore ribs when he did. "That little guy didn't do much damage."

"What happened to you?" Taylor was curious.

Jack was embarrassed to admit it but he was not going to lie to the man who had just saved his life. "Back in town a girl acted as a diversion and while my attention was on her a guy came up from behind and hit me over the head. He didn't knock me out but he dazed me enough to grab my wallet and take off with it."

"Okay." Taylor was confused. "So they left you behind. Where were you?"

"Outside the tavern where I was going to eat dinner."

"So how did you end up here?" Taylor pointed at the burning building.

"Maybe we should go someone else and cover that?" Jack suggested. The building was blazing by now and he didn't want to be standing around when people started showing up with questions.

"Alright then. We need to get our bearings then find out where The Mill is and get your property back." Taylor climbed in the car and started the engine.

"Right." Jack said as he got in the passenger side and put on his seatbelt. "By the way, I'm Jack." He stuck his hand out. "Thanks for saving my hide back there."

Taylor took Jack's hand and gave it a shake. "Taylor. Pleased to meet you, Jack." Then he grinned and added. "No thanks necessary because you know, I was in the neighborhood so…." They both laughed.

"Yeah, I'm actually very interested in hearing *that* story." Jack admitted.

Taylor steered the car back onto the road towards Green River. "Let's find a place in town where we can sit and talk. Maybe have some coffee or a bite to eat."

Jack nodded in agreement. *Man, what a weird night*, he thought.

They didn't have to drive too long before they saw a place to eat. They pulled up to a diner and went inside.

"I haven't eaten since lunch. You hungry, Jack?" Taylor asked as they walked up to the door.

Jack pulled his pockets inside out until the lining flapped over. "Flat broke, man." He sighed.

Taylor clapped him on the back. "No worries. I got this. Let's grab a bite and see if the locals will tell us anything about The Mill."

"Thanks. I already owe you my life. I guess just add dinner to my tab." Jack realized that sounded glib but how do you really pay someone back for saving you?

"I'm pretty sure you would have done the same thing in my shoes." Taylor told him as he slid into a booth.

Jack sat down across from him and picked up a menu. He hadn't eaten since lunch either and apparently you burn a lot of calories when someone is trying to kill you. He was hungry enough to eat the napkins out of the holder on the table. The two of them studied their menus in silence. When he was done, Jack closed his menu and watched the man across from him. He had no doubt he and Taylor would get his wallet back. His new friend looked pretty buff and based on what Jack had witnessed back at the Fina station, he had very little fear. The guy flat out walked through fire to save a total stranger.

"What can I get for you gentlemen?" The waitress asked placing two small glasses of ice water and two sets of utensils in front of them. Her name tag said that she was Kelley. She was a striking woman in her late 50's, her dark brown hair pulled back in a tight bun. She had soulful brown eyes and a warm smile. Taylor couldn't help but notice her big heart shaped earrings which swung like a pendulum each time she moved her head.

"Jack?" Taylor nodded toward his dinner companion.

"How are your burgers here, young lady?" Jack cocked his head to the side and raised an eyebrow.

Young lady, huh? Kelley was flattered. Jack was a handsome young man with enough charm to sell a snow cone to an Eskimo. She blushed and poised her pen over her order pad. "Well honey, it's no secret that Dean back there makes the best burgers in the county."

Jack nodded. "Sold!" he said. "I'll have a cheeseburger with everything on it and a side of fries. Oh, and a coke to drink." He tucked his menu back behind the napkin holder.

Kelley turned her attention to Taylor. "And for you, hon?" She enjoyed waiting on strangers passing through town. Seeing the same faces day after day got awful boring. It didn't hurt that these two were handsome as all get out.

Taylor was grinning at her as if he could read her mind. "Well, Kelley I think you sold me on that burger as well. Just give me the same as my friend here." He closed his menu and slid it in with the others.

"Two cheeseburgers with everything, two fries and two cokes." She repeated their order. "Anything else I can do for you two?" Her heart earrings swung wildly as she spoke.

"One thing. Would you happen to know anything about

The Mill?" Taylor asked.

Kelley gave it some thought. There were no bars or restaurants by that name in Green River. "I wish I could tell you but that's not ringing any bells with me. I'm sorry, hon."

"That's okay, Kelley. Thanks anyway." Taylor reached out and patted her arm. She couldn't help but giggle like a schoolgirl. Then he added, "Maybe you could ask Dean if he knows something about The Mill?" He flashed her the million-dollar smile.

"Let me get your order back to Dean and I'll see if he knows anything that can help you two." Kelley pivoted on her foot and swished her way back to the kitchen feeling 30 years younger.

Jack leaned in and said in a low voice, "I think she's sweet on you, big guy."

"Happens all the time." Taylor joked. He leaned back and put his hands behind his head, letting out a long sigh. "It's the price of being a chick magnet, my friend." He laughed and Jack joined in.

Jack liked this guy a lot. Not just because he saved his life, which was reason enough really. Not because he was buying him dinner and helping him get his wallet back. Taylor was a very friendly and likable person. He didn't take himself too seriously but at the same time he gave the impression he could definitely handle his business. He struck Jack as a genuinely good guy, a man who elicited trust. Having known Taylor for an hour at best, Jack felt so comfortable with him that it was like he was out having a bite with a life-long friend.

"Okay Jack." Taylor crossed his arms over his chest and raised one eyebrow. "Time to tell me how you went from getting rolled in a tavern parking lot to being tied up in a burning building."

Jack shook his head as if he couldn't believe the story he was about to tell. "After that guy knocked me in the head and they took off, I called a cab to take me back to the hotel. Can you believe I saw their truck at a convenience store as we were driving by?" He leaned in, eyes wide.

Taylor smiled. "What are the odds, right?"

"Well, I kind of wish now I hadn't seen them. But I did and I made the cab stop and let me out. I walked up to them and confronted them and POW! The guy landed a punch to my temple and I went out for quite a while I think."

"I can see the goose egg." Taylor pointed at Jack's head.

"Exactly." Jack touched the spot lightly and winced. "At some point I woke up sitting on the floor propped up against that pole with my hands tied. They took a few verbal jabs then the guy kicked the daylights out of my ribs and they left. But they came back with gas and matches and lit the place up. Just the icing on the cake I suppose."

"That's one bad night, my friend." Taylor said. "And it's not over yet. But I have a feeling it's going to take a turn for the better." He raised his water glass and Jack did likewise.

"Here's to turning this sinking ship around." Jack said and they touched the plastic water glasses making a dull clunk sound. Kelley showed up with their beverages and assured them their burgers would be out shortly.

"Okay, Sir. Your turn. How on God's green earth did YOU happen to show up out in the middle of nowhere just in time to walk through fire and save the day?" Jack wanted to know.

Taylor rested his arms on the table top and leaned in towards Jack. His expression was very serious. "You probably won't believe a word of what I'm about to tell you." He said in a low voice.

"I've experienced some pretty unbelievable things lately." Jack leaned in towards Taylor. "I might surprise you." He said.

Taylor thought about it. He got the impression that Jack was a level headed and open minded person.

"Do you believe in God, Jack?" Taylor began.

"Yes I do." Jack answered, his face lighting up immediately. Taylor noticed the instant brightening of Jack's expression when he mentioned God. This might not be as hard to explain as he had feared.

"Me too." Taylor said. "In fact, I am extremely in tune with Him lately and because I am actively listening, He is getting through when he wants to 'speak' to me. Does that make sense?"

"It makes perfect sense." Jack was smiling and nodding. "God is always speaking to us, we're just too busy or distracted to hear His voice sometimes."

Taylor opened his mouth to speak but stopped when he felt an intense tingly feeling from head to toe at the same time a warm breeze jetted passed the booth. Jack turned his head as if watching something streak by.

"Did you feel that?" Jack asked, wide-eyed.

Taylor nodded and looked around. No one else seemed to notice anything. "I sure did!" He said a little breathless. "But I think we are the only ones who did."

"What's going on?" Jack was confused but excited. Something was happening and it was because of the topic they were discussing. He was sure of it.

"Whatever it was, it wasn't anything bad." Taylor

observed. "You didn't feel anything negative, did you?"

"Far from it." Jack was grinning. "Something wonderful just rushed by."

"I got the same feeling and I don't think it is gone." Taylor shrugged.

Jack scanned the dining room. He didn't see anything unusual. "Now that you mention it, I can still feel it but it's like I'm becoming more used to it being here. Like I'm acclimating."

"Me too." Taylor agreed. Kelley arrived with their food and after giving thanks, they dug into their meals. The burgers were everything Kelley had promised. Even the fries were exceptional.

"Do you think the food is better because of whatever came in?" Jack joked between bites.

"Nothing would surprise me these days." Taylor confided. He realized he never finished explaining how he came to find Jack in the middle of nowhere, but it didn't feel like the right time to explain.

Jack suspected that meeting Taylor was no accident and that every move he had made had led him to this night to meet this man. Now the why was what had him really curious. He had no idea that across the table, Taylor was having the exact same thought. It hadn't escaped Taylor's attention that when he rolled into town and was closer in proximity to Jack, his intuition, awareness and feeling of purpose all increased dramatically. He felt virtually no fear at all when he walked through the flames and broke that window. Everything was coming together and walking with the supernatural seemed to be part of the package.

They finished their meals with no room for dessert so both declined when Kelley asked if they wanted to try Dean's fabulous apple pie. She gave them the bad news that Dean had not heard of any place called The Mill either. They thanked her again for asking then Taylor paid the check and left Kelley a tip that made her legs wobbly. But it was something else that made her take a seat later as she counted out the cash. Taylor had jotted a note for her on the ticket which simply said, "Tell him tonight." She looked over at the kitchen where Dean was working busily.

Kelley and Dean had worked together in this place for over 5 years. They were both single and had enjoyed a flirtatious friendship. Recently Kelley had come face to face with the fact that she was actually very deeply in love with Dean but she had no idea what to do about it. She was terrified to tell him how she felt. Hadn't she just been thinking about it that afternoon before she came in to work? No, thinking wasn't the right word. She had sat in her car in the parking lot, wringing her apron in her hands asking God what to do. Now there was this note. Its meaning was unmistakable.

She sat and pondered the situation for a while then stood up and smoothed out her apron. It was late and the last of the customers had left. She walked over to the door and flipped the CLOSED sign around and turned the lock on the door. Then Kelley took the advice Taylor had given her and walked confidently to the kitchen. She tapped Dean on the shoulder and he turned around with a big smile.

"Yessum?" He said, making her heart pound a million miles per hour.

"Dean Jessup, I love you. I have for about as long as I can remember." She announced with her hands on her hips.

"How 'bout that?" He said putting his spatula down. He wiped his hands with a rag and reached into his pocket as he lowered onto one knee. "Took you long enough." He opened the tiny box he held in his hand. His eyes welled up with tears. "Kelley

Marie Patterson, will you do me the honor of being my wife?"
Kelley's legs failed her at that moment and she too was soon down
on the floor, momentarily struck dumb with shock.

"Is this happening?" She choked the words out.

"I've been carrying this ring to work every day for 2 years,
just waiting for a sign." His voice was thick with emotion. "I've
loved you from the first moment I saw you, woman. But I didn't
think I had a chance with you."

She threw her arms around him and covered his face with
kisses. "You, silly old goat! Yes! I will be your wife!" He slipped
the ring on her finger and then told her he would prepare a special
dinner for two to celebrate. While he was cooking she reached into
her apron pocket and took the ticket Taylor had written his
message on. She kissed the words he had scribbled and praised
God over and over as she watched the love of her life with brand
new eyes.

CHAPTER 18

Taylor and Jack left the diner and walked across the parking lot to the car when they noticed someone leaning against the back of the Maxima. She appeared to be in her 20's with reddish brown hair styled in a short pixie cut. She was very cute with fair skin, large round eyes and small slightly turned up nose. She was petite and slender, wearing jeans, a white tank top and flip flops. Her ankles were crossed as were her arms and she greeted them with a huge grin.

"May I help you, Miss?" Taylor asked as he and Jack approached. Jack was on guard immediately, which was understandable considering what he had been through earlier. He kept his distance and was watchful for any movement around them.

"Hi fellas." She said. "I overheard you asking Kelley about The Mill." She nodded towards the diner.

Taylor spoke up immediately. "You know something?" He took a few steps closer.

"Sure do and I can take you there." She offered. Her tone and manner were friendly. "You're obviously not from around here so I doubt you would find it by yourself no matter how good my directions are."

"That's a fair assumption. We will follow you then." Taylor suggested.

"Sorry, no car. I'm on foot." She shrugged. "Give me a ride and I can show you where it is. I will go my own way after we get there. I can get a ride back into town later."

Something about this didn't sit well with Taylor. First the girl was perfectly willing to get into a car with two strange men which was dangerous and irresponsible. Second, she could potentially be stuck at this mill place without any way of getting back home, just taking her chances that someone trustworthy would get her home safe. Was she naïve or just incredibly brave? She didn't look frail or weak but she was small and could easily be overpowered by someone bigger than her. Suddenly he got a crazy notion in his head. What if she was Rose? Could it possibly be that easy?

"That's nice of you to make the offer. I'm sorry, what is your name, Miss?"

"I'm Caroline." She smiled revealing perfectly straight white teeth. Her smile was electrifying and gave Taylor a feeling of euphoria. It was a very strange and wonderful quality. Of course, Taylor could not help feeling a little disappointed that she didn't introduce herself as Rose. But did it matter, really? His mission had not changed and helping Jack get his wallet back was important as well. If Caroline could help, who was he to say no?

"I'm Taylor and this is Jack."

Caroline turned to Jack. "You're the quiet one, huh?"

"Sometimes." He eyed her suspiciously.

"I don't remember seeing you inside, Caroline." Taylor admitted.

"That's funny because I remember seeing *you*." Her expression became serious as she looked Taylor in the eyes and held his gaze for a moment. Then the next instant she was smiling and playful again. "I was at the counter enjoying a piece of pie and a glass of milk." She explained. "You missed out by skipping dessert. Dean's apple pie is amazing."

It took Taylor a moment to recover from Caroline's penetrating eyes. He felt a little off balance, but forced himself to focus. "We appreciate your help." Taylor started towards the Maxima. "Hop in you two and let's get this show on the road."

Once she had them going in the right direction, Taylor pressed her for more information. "Is this a bar or a club?"

"Yes and no." She leaned up from the back seat until she was right between Jack and Taylor with her elbows on the center console. "It's an outdoor gathering place tucked away and private. There's a patio with a fire pit and some chairs. Mostly kids who bring their own coolers and maybe they share their beverages and snacks, maybe they don't. Folks park off the main road and walk through some trees to the spot. It isn't too far from the road but well hidden from anyone who is just passing by."

"And why is it called The Mill?" Jack was curious.

"The land belongs to Jayce Miller." She explained and pointed to the left. "Turn here." She told Taylor. "Jayce set it up so people can party out there as long as they don't fight or trash the place. Anyone who has had too much to drink is encouraged to stay and sleep it off there on the property until they are sober. It used to be called Miller's Place but over time it just became known as The Mill." She pointed again. "Make a right up there."

"What are the odds we'll remember how to get out of this place?" Jack mused.

Taylor glanced over at him and winked. "Not to worry, my friend. I'm making a mental roadmap as we go. I'm like MapQuest. When we leave I'll hit the 'reverse directions' button in my head and we'll have no problems at all."

Jack looked at Taylor and nodded wondering if he was serious or joking. It wasn't easy to tell the difference. He decided that was part of Taylor's charm. He was good natured and an eternal optimist if ever Jack had seen one. A few more turns until Caroline told them to pull off the road and head down a narrow dirt path that seemingly stopped at a thicket of trees. She pointed out an opening and when they cleared the curtain of foliage they were in a huge open area with a couple of dozen cars and trucks. Jack could barely make out the flicker of a fire through the trees that flanked the parking area. And there they were. They had found The Mill.

As soon as the car came to a stop, Caroline jumped out but she leaned in before closing the door. "I'm going to go see what's up. I don't know what your plans are here so I'll just say it was a pleasure and I'll see you around sometime." With that she flashed a smile and sprinted off through the trees and disappeared.

"I think we need to come up with a plan." Jack turned to Taylor as he killed the engine.

"Great idea. I'm all ears." Taylor said with a sheepish grin.

Jack laughed nervously. "I was hoping *you* had one."

Taylor leaned back against the headrest and closed his eyes. "Well, partner today is your lucky day because it just so happens that I do."

Relief swept over Jack. "Thank God."

Taylor opened his eyes and stared straight ahead. "So, what do we know about the people who attacked you?"

"That they are evil?" Jack guessed.

"Well yeah, but I was thinking that they know what *you* look like. I think you should change into something else and wear a baseball cap and these." He held up his sunglasses.

"Problem." Jack sighed. "All my clothes are back at the

125

hotel in Green River."

"Problem solved." Taylor hit the trunk button and the back lid swung open. "I didn't make it to a hotel yet so all my stuff is in the trunk. Open my suitcase and change your shirt and grab a hat. I need you to keep a low profile and ID them for me. Then we'll follow them back to their car when they leave and we'll get your wallet back. Easy peazy."

Jack was impressed. "Simple yet brilliant." He said as he got out of the car and went back to the trunk to rummage through Taylor's clothing.

Taylor rolled his window down but remained in the car and closed his eyes. "Lord, I don't know what this has to do with Rose but I know your hand is in this so I'm trusting you to help us." He prayed.

"What's that?" Jack called out from behind the car.

"Sorry. Talking to someone else, " Taylor apologized.

Jack found a button-down shirt to wear over the tee shirt he had on when those bozos jacked his wallet and tied him up. He put it on and buttoned the shirt quickly then found a baseball cap. That should do the trick. Jeans were jeans and there was nothing special about his sneakers so he felt pretty good about his disguise. He tucked in the shirt and went back to the driver's side of the car. Taylor handed him the sunglasses through the open window.

He grinned as he hiked the waist of his jeans up really high and assumed a posture that made him look like Carl in the movie, Sling Blade. "I hope I can get me some biscuits and mustard in there, mm hmm." He did a perfect impersonation.

Taylor laughed. He really liked this kid and he reminded him so much of Brian. He estimated that Jack was about the same age Brian would be today had he lived.

"I like the way you talk." Taylor played along with an exaggerated southern accent as he got out and locked the car.

"Me and you made *friends*, mm hmm." Jack stayed in character. "Let's go find us some French-fried puh-taters." He turned and started walking just like the character in the movie.

"Wait up, will you?" Taylor chuckled.

When Jack turned around his bottom lip was pulled up over his top lip and his chin thrust out as he made grunting noises. "Well c'mon then, mmm hmmm."

"Okay, okay, we need to get serious." Taylor laughed.

Jack pulled the waist of his jeans back down to the proper height and stood up straight. He put the sunglasses on and they walked through the trees and stepped right into The Mill.

When they entered from the grove of trees there was a wide flat stone pathway lined with small lights which led to a larger three-tiered patio. It was paved with the same flat smooth stone. The first level was one step up. The second level was offset to the back left of the first level and the third was offset to the right and was a bi-level area which could be accessed by going up two steps from the first level or one step up from the second level. The perimeter of each separate level was partly surrounded by a short stone wall which was the perfect height for seating. The only part without a wall was about ¼ of each level that was open for entry. A large pergola was the focal point at the back of the third level. Decorative party lanterns hung from beams to illuminate the seating area where there were large, extra wide loungers filled with pillows. There was a small fire pit under the pergola plenty of distance from the loungers.

There was a huge fire pit in the middle of the first level surrounded by several dozen Adirondack chairs painted a multitude of colors. On the right was a bar covered with various kinds of snacks with a keg placed at one end. The second level is where all the coolers were tucked away underneath or near the dozen or so wrought iron patio tables. The coolers varied from small styrofoam boxes to very large elaborate chests. Music poured out from outdoor speakers which were located in key areas around the patio, some mounted on trees and some affixed to the upright posts of the pergola. The source of the music was well-hidden because there was no obvious indication where the stereo components were located.

Jack elbowed Taylor and nodded towards the bar. He started walking that direction and Taylor followed. There were five people at the bar at that moment. Three were getting snacks, one behind the bar was complaining because she couldn't find a bottle opener and one was trying to work the keg. Jack turned his back on them when he was 8-10 feet away and leaned in to whisper to Taylor. "The girl behind the bar and the guy piling Cheetos on his plate."

Taylor took a moment to size them up then nodded. He and Jack walked over to the pergola where they found Caroline by the fire pit jumping up and down to the rhythm of the dance music. She had the attention of several men in the area as she danced with abandon, her body keeping perfect rhythm with the music. Her eyes were closed and she had the tiniest upward curve on her lips. It wasn't so much a smile as an expression of absolute contentment. Oblivious to the world around her, she was lost in the music.

Jack put his hand on Taylor's shoulder which startled him. "Clearly not her first rodeo." He said, nodding in her direction.

"I don't like the way that guy is looking at her." Taylor gestured towards a heavy set young male wearing a dark hoodie with a pentagram on the front. The logo was dripping blood. He was watching Caroline like a man on a mission. The sight of it sent a chill through him.

"He's probably harmless." Jack said. "Here." He handed Taylor a bottle of water.

"Where did you find this?" Taylor looked around.

"Stashed in a built-in cooler behind the bar." He said and took a long draw on his own bottle. "This setup isn't too shabby, man." He said as he took it all in.

"So, I noticed." Taylor agreed. "She down-played it quite a bit didn't she?" He held his water bottle out towards Caroline. At that very moment, she opened her eyes and looked right at Taylor and flashed a big smile. He took an involuntary step backwards and almost lost his balance. She giggled and raised her arms over her head and danced in a circle turning her back on him.

Jack guided Taylor around so Caroline would be behind him. "We need to stay focused, big guy." He said with both hands on Taylor's shoulders.

Taylor shook his head as if to clear his mind. "You're right. "He looked over Jack's shoulder. "Let's keep a close eye on them. Do you think he has your wallet or would the girl have it?"

"He does, or at least he did." Jack answered. "I saw him stuff it in his back pocket when he took it from me. From the looks of his two bulging back pockets it's still there."

"Makes sense." Taylor agreed. The two of them were next to the large fire pit on level one chatting with a group of people. "Stay here." Taylor instructed Jack and walked away. He walked towards the culprits very slowly and hung out close by making it look as if he were chatting with other people on the fringe of their group.

He blended in well from where Jack stood. Jack watched the guy who had his wallet gesturing wildly as if re-enacting a fight. It dawned on him that he was bragging about what he'd done to Jack earlier. Taylor was easing in closer by the minute. Finally, he was right there mingling next to the rather animated story-teller and his audience. Taylor had adopted their posture and mannerisms and in a very short time he had become impossible to distinguish from the rest of the crowd. Taylor was smiling and nodding as he effortlessly blended in with the group. Jack shook his head and smiled. He sat down on the stone wall and watched his friend in action. Taylor said something and everyone laughed.

Taylor infiltrated their group with an ease that could only be attributed to divine intervention. His heart was pounding wildly as the guy that had tried to kill Jack was telling the story about what he'd done to some stupid outsider who came into his territory. Taylor was pretty sure the story was grossly exaggerated but only Jack could testify to that. At one point, Taylor interjected without thinking.

"What a loser!" Taylor commented.

"Exactly!" The guy lifted his beer bottle to Taylor in salute. Taylor raised his water bottle.

"Water? Really?" The guy looked at Taylor suspiciously.

"Pfft! Try Grey Goose, little man." Taylor informed him. Everyone raised their hands to high five Taylor, including the storyteller. Taylor thought his heart might explode. Grey Goose? Good grief! Who had he turned into?

Jack watched everyone high fiving Taylor and he wished he could hear what was being said. Clearly the man who had saved his life had some serious skills.

"Aww, your friend left you all alone." A voice startled him. Jack turned and there was Caroline sitting next to him.

"He's a social butterfly." Jack shrugged. "What's a boy to do?"

"You don't say much but when you do I've noticed it is always sarcasm."

Jack turned towards her with a wounded look on his face. He touched his hand to his heart. "That hurts me. Deeply." He said in a sad little voice.

"I rest my case" She stood up quickly.

"Well, I aim to please." He said flatly.

"Hmmm. You say one thing but you mean the exact opposite." She put her hands on her hips, cocked her head to the side and smirked at him.

"Interesting observation." He said.

She laughed. "And there it is again. You say interesting but you mean that it's anything but interesting."

"You have a point?" Jack sighed, unamused by her antics. Perhaps another time and place he would have found her somewhat charming but he was here on business and she was annoying. Besides that, he was admittedly jaded after his recent experiences with her gender.

"You two are up to something." Her expression went from playful to serious in an instant. "I'm getting a hardcore Mission Impossible vibe from you guys."

"You're drunk." Jack dismissed her.

"Haven't had a drop." She said as she raised her arms in the air and shimmied to the music. "Come dance with me Jack."

"If it will shut you up then yes." Jack followed her to the fire pit near where Taylor was.

Taylor saw Jack and Caroline over by the fire pit, dancing. Caroline was having fun but Jack looked annoyed. Taylor caught his eye and Jack shrugged. Taylor stuck his tongue out making Jack laugh. *Keep it together. We're almost done here,* Taylor thought. Jack nodded as if reading Taylor's mind.

Jack kept his eyes on Taylor who apparently won the trust of the bad guy/story-teller. Taylor said something to him and the two of them turned and walked towards the trees. Taylor glanced over his shoulder at Jack and nodded once. Jack understood that to mean *follow, but stay out of sight.*

He turned to Caroline. "Stay here."

Jack watched as Taylor and the bad guy disappeared through the trees. He followed but hung back behind the cover of the trees. They stopped when they reached a white pickup truck which was the bad guy's vehicle. Taylor reached back under his jacket and pulled something from his waistband. Taylor had a gun? Jack gasped then clamped his hand over his mouth to keep quiet. He watched Taylor shove what looked like a gun against the guy's neck and up went the bad man's hands. Taylor said something then pulled the wallet from the guy's back pocket. He opened it and looked inside as best he could with one hand. The hand holding the wallet motioned for Jack to come on.

"You know, it is times like this when life and death hang in the balance that you should ask yourself if anything you are doing is making your life better." Taylor said to the guy. "I mean if I were in your shoes, I would take a moment to think about what my fate will be when the police find a dead body in a burned up gas

132

station on the outskirts of Green River. A body that was once a living breathing person that witnesses saw YOU and your girlfriend drag into that building, tie up and then leave for dead as you set a fire and drove away.

The guy whimpered something unintelligible.

"And another thing. Living in the age of technology, it is reasonable to assume that the witnesses got you on video doing the deed." Taylor shoved the gun into the guy's neck even harder for emphasis.

"What do you want from me?" The guy cried.

"I'm taking this wallet to the police myself so they can identify the body." Taylor told him as he shoved the wallet into his jacket pocket. "Is everything still in it?"

"Yes!" The guy said." We came straight here after. We didn't take anything out, I swear!"

"Good." Taylor pushed the guy up against his truck. "Where's your phone?"

"In my front pocket." He groaned.

"Which one?" Taylor demanded.

"Left! My left pocket!"

"See how easy things are when you cooperate? So here's what's going to happen." Taylor reached into the guy's left pocket and retrieved the phone. "I'm going to dial 911. Then I'm going to hold it up for you and you're going to tell them what you did, where to find the body and where you are right now."

"Please no." The guy begged.

"Or I can just shoot you in the back of the head." Taylor said matter-of-factly. "Since I'm feeling generous, I'll let you decide."

"Phone." The guy said, sobbing now.

"Excellent choice." Taylor said. He dialed 911 and held the phone up to the guy's ear.

"911, what is your emergency?" The voice said when the call connected.

"I…Um.." The guy stammered in between sobs.

"Shall I cock this thing?" Taylor asked him."

The guy suddenly found his words. "I need to report a murder." He said. "I mean, I want to confess!"

"What is your name sir?" The 911 operator asked.

"Billy Perkins." He told the operator.

"And where is the victim?"

"In the old abandoned Fina station on Johnson Bridge Road." He said. "I set a fire and burned the guy up."

"Where are you calling from now, Mr. Perkins?"

"I'm at The Mill. Um, Jayce Miller's place." Billy said.

"Units are on the way." The operator said. "Please wait there until they arrive."

Taylor took the phone and ended the call. "Nice job, Billy." He said. You did the right thing. Believe it or not, this will turn out to be good for you."

"I doubt that." Billy sobbed.

"I'm going to leave now, Billy." Taylor said. "We never met."

"What?" Billy was confused.

"I said, we never met!" Taylor shoved the gun deeper into Billy's neck. "You don't want me coming back to execute the other option do you?"

"No!" Billy screamed. "No! We never met! You were never here!"

"That's a good boy, Billy." Taylor said. "Stay where you are and don't move until the police arrive. And don't turn around." He tossed Billy's cell phone into the trees. "And don't yell for help. Where are your truck keys, Billy?"

"Oh man!" Billy protested.

"Billy…" Taylor pressed the gun in hard again.

"Okay! Okay!" Billy wailed. "They are in my right pocket!"

Taylor reached into Billy's right pocket and took his keys and held onto them.

"Okay, I'm leaving you now." Taylor said. He could hear sirens in the distance. "You should be proud that you are doing the right thing." With that Taylor backed away and motioned for Jack to join him. They climbed into the Maxima and Taylor eased them out of the parking area slowly and quietly without drawing any attention to their departure.

****

Billy waited alone by his truck as the police sirens grew closer. He shook his head as if coming out of a dream. *Oh my God!* He thought. *I've killed someone!* Suddenly Billy was terrified. What had he been thinking when he jumped that guy at the tavern? Admittedly, he wasn't above taking advantage of an unlocked car and boosting a radio but hitting a guy over the head and robbing him? He couldn't remember if it had been his idea or Brenda's to put the bait of a woman in trouble out there to lure him in. And why this particular guy? It was weird how all that seemed to happen in a haze. By the time they had stopped to tie down the fishing gear that was rattling around in the bed of the truck, he had all but forgotten about the guy. Billy never even thought about what happened next – clocking the guy again hard enough to knock him out when he approached them and then driving him out to the old Fina station and tying him up. It felt like it happened to someone else. Now he was piecing together what he had done but couldn't remember what had motivated him, especially setting fire to the place. And what was up with bragging about it to everyone at The Mill?

Billy jumped when Brenda appeared next to him. "What were we thinking?" He asked her.

"What are you talking about?" She stepped back and took a defensive posture.

"Killing that guy?" He was crying again. "Who thought that was a good idea?"

"Yeah, like you don't remember, Billy." She shrugged.

"That's BS, Brenda." He said. "We're in the tavern and the next thing I know you're playing damsel in distress and I jump some stranger from behind. Who does that?"

"Where have *you* been?" She gave him a look of concern.

"What?" Billy demanded.

"Hello? That creepy dude that sat down with us at the bar? He has everything to do with this." She reminded him.

"Huh?" Billy was lost.

"What is wrong with you?" She screamed at him. "Are you stupid?"

"No, I'm not! I just don't know what you are talking about!" He screamed back at her.

"Let me dumb it down for you then. While we were at the bar a guy with short black hair came up and started talking to us. He was kind of cute except his eyebrows looked like fuzzy black caterpillars. I could have sworn I saw them moving too. It was super creepy. He said a lot really weird stuff that didn't make any sense and then suddenly you were all 'Yeah man, let's do this!' Then he told us exactly what to do step by step and who to wait for." She put her finger in Billy's face. "And it was YOUR idea to go along with him!" She punched him in the arm as hard as she could. "I only cooperated because you said if I didn't you'd just leave me there and we would be history."

Suddenly it all came rushing back to him. The guy had introduced himself as Berk and somehow, he had put Billy in some kind of trance. He also remembered that same guy showed up at the Fina station and handed him the full can of gas and a book of matches. He reached into his pocket and pulled out the matchbook. It was black with a raised red pentagram on it but nothing else.

"He tricked me so it's not my fault!" He said finally, throwing the matchbook at Brenda. It made him feel a little better but not much.

"Whatever." Brenda said. She picked up the matchbook, tossed it into the open window of Billy's truck and it landed on the floor. "And if the cops are coming for you, you are on your own, Jerk." She turned and walked back through the trees into the Mill.

The sirens were very close now and he could see the flashing lights through the trees. He slid down the side of his truck, landed on his backside on the ground and cried. No way would the cops believe he had been hypnotized by some weirdo who came up to him at the tavern and told him to do bad things. As his daddy was fond of saying, his goose was cooked.

****

They sat in silence until they were on the main road then Jack turned to Taylor.

"You have a gun?" Jack blurted out, clearly astonished.

Taylor laughed. "Sure." He tossed it to Jack who screamed like a girl and caught it with both hands. He stared in disbelief at the small black metal flashlight in his hands. The cylinder looked enough like the barrel of a gun to fool anyone. "Grabbed this from the console before I got out back at the mill." The brilliance of Taylor's bluff hit Jack like a ton of bricks.

"You are the man!" Jack yelled. He rolled his window down and shouted outside. "Taylor is... THE MAN! Wooooo!"

"Oh stop." Taylor chuckled and rolled Jack's window up. "I'm not even sure how any of that happened." He admitted.

"What do you mean? You were amazing!"

"I mean, it was like someone else took over and I was watching it all happen from the sidelines." Taylor gave Jack a serious look. "Nothing like that has ever happened to me before."

"Well you are a natural then because you pulled that off like a boss!"

"Thanks." He chuckled and handed Jack his wallet. "At least we got your wallet back."

"Thanks Taylor!" Jack was beaming.

"And I think we can get rid of these." Taylor handed Billy's truck keys to Jack and rolled his window down. Jack tossed them out the window and into the ditch on the side of the road.

"Mission accomplished" Taylor yawned. "Can we call it a night now?"

"I have a room at the hotel on Main." Jack said. "You're welcome crash there if you want."

"I'll take you up on that offer." Taylor said and drove to the hotel where Jack was staying.

CHAPTER 19

The alarm went off at 8:30 am the next morning. It seemed to Taylor as if he had only just closed his eyes. He let Jack sleep while he went into the bathroom to shower, shave, and get ready for the day. He saw the complimentary coffee pot and started a brew.

The smell of brewing coffee roused Jack from his sleep at 9:05. Taylor was already dressed and reading his Bible. That made Jack smile. He stretched and sat up. "Morning'" he said.

"Good morning to you." Taylor set his Bible aside. "You get enough sleep, buddy?" He asked.

"I think so." Jack stood up and stretched again. "I feel pretty good all things considered. Coffee smells great."

"Freshly brewed for your pleasure, sir." Taylor said in a snooty butler voice.

"Very good, Jeeves." Jack joked and waved dismissively. "That will be all."

Taylor bowed and grinned. "It's actually in the bathroom. Kind of weird but I can't really find fault with free coffee."

"Same here." Jack said and shuffled off to the bathroom, returning shortly with a steaming cup. "So Taylor, what's next for you?"

Taylor, sipping his cup of coffee, stopped and looked at Jack with an eyebrow raised. "Good question. How about you?"

Jack told Taylor about his plan for cross country travel by greyhound. He shrugged. "I guess I'll just catch the next bus." He said.

"You're welcome to ride with me." Taylor said. "I'm headed east and so are you."

"If you're sure it wouldn't be an imposition."

"Actually, I would enjoy the company."

Jack really liked Taylor and he thought traveling together would be fun and based on the previous night, it could prove more of an adventure than anything he would experience by bus. "Sounds great, Taylor." Jack took his coffee and headed for the bathroom to shower and get ready.

Taylor picked up his Bible, but didn't read right away. Instead he closed his eyes and prayed for wisdom and guidance on how to communicate with Jack about the rose business. He wasn't sure how much God wanted him to share.

Thirty minutes later Jack checked out of the hotel and found Taylor waiting by his car. When he started the engine, the radio came on to the Third Day song, *Everywhere You Go*.

"Is this okay, or do you want me to change it to another station?" Taylor asked, the lyrics to the song not escaping his notice.

Jack laughed. "This is my music, man. Contemporary Christian. I play and sing at church. Well, I did back home anyways."

"Why am I not surprised?" Taylor smiled and turned up the volume as he steered the car out of the parking lot and onto the road leading to the interstate.

Taylor said, "You told me you were seeing the country by bus on your way to Boston for a new job." Then added, "I'm curious. Why did you decide to travel by bus instead of taking a plane?"

"When I initially accepted the job, flying out was the plan. I would leave the week before my start date and get settled in." He shrugged. "But then I read an article about this guy who had the time of his life seeing the country by greyhound. It occurred to me that I had never really done anything spontaneous in my life. I felt a strong conviction that this was the route I needed to take, so I did the unthinkable and changed my play-it-safe plans."

"So, has it been everything you hoped for so far?" Taylor was curious.

"Funny you should ask." Jack found Taylor very easy to talk to. He told him about the breakup with Danielle and his encounter with Hailey on the bus to Salt Lake City. All the while Taylor listened, genuinely interested. He asked lots of questions and made observations. His warm nature reminded Jack of everything he wished his own father had been. He wanted to ask if Taylor had kids, but right now he felt like the timing was wrong.

"And after you got to Salt Lake City?" Taylor asked.

"I did a lot of touristy things. Sight-seeing mostly." Jack responded but something about his tone struck Taylor as odd.

"But..." Taylor prompted.

Jack took the bait. "But... something strange did happen my last day there." He went on to describe the event in the park with the boy. "I got the feeling that the security guard was hell bent on detaining me. Like his mission in life was to lock me up and keep me there. I know that sounds paranoid." Jack said, embarrassed.

"Maybe not." Taylor had an uneasy feeling. "You said you had not seen any security guards around there at any time before or after, right?"

"Correct."

"And he appeared seemingly out of nowhere the instant the mother came into view screaming?"

"That's right."

"Was there anything else unusual about the security guard?"

"His attitude towards the other guy - the witness, Jordan. It was unusually hostile. I couldn't help but feel like these two had history. Like there was bad blood between them. Supposedly they were total strangers but standing between them it felt like anything but that." Jack struggled to find the right words to explain what it was like. "You are a man of faith. I know you've felt the presence of good around you before, right? I mean we just encountered something like that at the diner." Taylor nodded yes. "So I guess the question is, have you ever felt the presence of something truly evil?"

Taylor recalled the encounter with "Karen" the night before he left. She had been sweet at first, trying to convince him to stay. Then she turned hostile. He definitely felt the presence of evil then. Again Taylor nodded yes to Jack's question.

"Well then I guess the best way to describe how I felt was that it was like standing in the middle of a showdown between good and evil, where the two are battling for something. I know this sounds nuts and I can't blame you if you think I'm crazy, but at the time it really felt like I was the prize to be won or lost between Jordan who was good and Sully who was evil." Jack shook his head and laughed nervously. "Geez, saying it out loud like that it sounds crazy to me and I was there."

In an instant, Taylor had 100% clarity about the situation. "You aren't crazy, Jack. What you are is very perceptive." Taylor assured him. "That feeling that you were a prize to be won or lost

143

is accurate. You were. Well, you ARE. That man Sully was on a mission to detain you. And that's not the end of it. The guy who took your wallet and tried to kill you was on the same mission, whether he was consciously aware of it or just influenced to target you." He looked over at Jack and saw him looking back wide eyed, mouth hanging open. "They didn't want us to find each other, Jack. I'm certain of it. Did this Jordan guy say anything to you afterwards?" Taylor would have bet everything that he did.

"Yes." Jack replied slowly. "I was about to thank him for what he had done and he told me there was no need, that I was being set up. I tried to explain that I didn't know any of those people and didn't understand why they would want to set me up. He said it didn't matter, that THEY know me." He remembered how he felt that little surge of electricity when Jordan had put his hand on his shoulder. "Then he told me to be careful because that was just the beginning."

Taylor felt no fear, only adrenaline coursing through his body. That all too familiar voice spoke from inside his head. "Tell him now." It insisted and Taylor understood it was time to tell Jack everything. He started from the beginning just as he had done when he met Marvin Petros. He told Jack about the headaches, the voices, the red hue, the strange events, including the dog, the message at church and the rose. Jack sat completely silent the entire time taking it all in. It was impossible for Taylor to gauge whether or not Jack believed him but he was telling him everything regardless. "And I was unexpectedly delayed too, but strangely enough, the result was that the delay *caused* me to be in the right place at the right time to find you." He told Jack how his car wouldn't start but nothing was wrong with it and about Weldon, the tow truck driver. "There are no mistakes, Jack." He said when he was finished.

"You're right about that." Jack said soberly. "Taylor, I dreamed of an enormous garden of red roses. When I woke up, I could still smell them."

Taylor took his foot off the gas pedal and pulled the car onto the shoulder. He threw it in park and turned to face Jack. "When did this happen?" He watched as Jack mentally reviewed the week and when he found the day he looked over at Taylor and opened his mouth but no sound came out. He looked terrified. Finally, he found his voice.

"I woke up that morning smelling roses in my room, the day I met Jordan and Sully in the park." He swallowed hard and rolled down the window for some air. "What does this mean?"

Taylor's mind was racing. So Jack was having visions about Rose as well. He now believed that Jack was one of the people God had told him He would send. '…trust Me and I will provide everything and *everyone* you need'. He shared this observation with Jack who was still trying to wrap his head around the whole thing.

"Taylor, I believe everything you told me. I believe you have been given a huge responsibility. I just wasn't prepared that I might also be…" His voice trailed off.

"Entrusted by God to do something truly significant?" Taylor finished. He put his hand on Jack's shoulder. That fatherly gesture alone was all it took to open the floodgates. Suddenly he was spilling his guts about his childhood, his mother and his father. He didn't realize how close to the surface his feelings were until Taylor had shown up in his life.

"Do you think you can reconcile with your father?" Taylor asked. He had merged the Maxima back into the flow of traffic onto the interstate while Jack was talking about his life.

"That bridge was burned when he slept with the girl I was getting ready to propose to." Jack admitted.

Taylor felt Jack's pain from where he sat. "That's pretty rough, man."

"When I was a teenager, I had this crazy idea that by some miracle I'd have a close relationship with him by the time I was in my twenties. You know, an easy kind of rapport like close friends." He paused. "Like you and I have."

"You are searching for your father." Taylor spoke in a voice that sounded very far away. "And I am searching for my son."

"Do you have kids, Taylor?" Jack saw his opening and took it.

"I did." Taylor answered, coming back to himself again. "A son, Brian. He died seven years ago."

"How old was he?"

"He was 20 when he died." Taylor said.

"So, he'd be 27 now?" Jack asked.

"Yes. And if I were a betting man, I'd say that's your age right now." Taylor glanced over at Jack who was looking back at him nodding yes.

"What happened?" Jack asked. "If you don't mind telling me, that is."

"He was driving home from work one night and a drunk driver hit him head on. They say he died instantly and didn't suffer." Taylor paused.

"And your wife?" Jack asked cautiously.

"Karen was destroyed by Brian's death. She lost her faith and became angry with God." Taylor recalled. "She began to self-medicate with alcohol and later added pills to the mix. For two years she did this and the entire time I tried everything I could think of to pull her out of it. But she was lost to the darkness and she was determined to self-destruct. Two years later to the day Brian died she died from a lethal interaction of alcohol and pills. I found her in our bed when I came home from work."

Jack waited a bit before he asked, "Do you think it was intentional?"

Taylor shook his head. "I really can't say for sure. I never thought she was the kind of person who could do that…" He shrugged. "…but then again, maybe she wanted the pain to end more than she wanted to live."

"I'm sorry I made you talk about it." Jack said, feeling deep sorrow for Taylor.

"She died five years ago. I've come to terms with it by now. Don't feel bad."

Jack mentally ran through all the events that led the two of them to this moment. There was his loss of a father and Taylor's loss of a son. Now they find each other. It was overwhelming, amazing and humbling.

They rode in silence for a while then Jack spoke up changing the subject. "So much has happened in such a short span of time, but I'm more curious than ever about what that was at the diner. That odd tingly feeling when that warm gust of air blew passed us."

"And what about the girl who just *happened* to be waiting to help us outside?" Taylor added. "Did YOU see her in the diner at any point? Because I didn't."

"No. She wasn't in there. I was watching everyone in the diner at the counter and everywhere else. I was so rattled by what had happened to me earlier that night that I was looking out for any other threats that might come out of nowhere. She wasn't in the diner having pie. She lied."

"So, the question is, who is she?" Taylor mused. "And what is her agenda?"

"She's annoying but I don't think she's a bad guy." Jack smiled remembering how irritating she was. Hard to believe that could almost be an endearing quality. She was ridiculously cute even though she was a brat.

Reflecting on what Taylor had told him, this was going to be dangerous but whether he liked it or not Jack was all in. This didn't seem like a voluntary kind of deal. He had been drafted into the role. He suddenly began to laugh hysterically. Taylor looked at him with an amused expression.

"Something I said?" Taylor asked.

"No!" Jack sputtered as he laughed even harder. "I left home hoping for an interesting experience."

Taylor burst out laughing. "Well you got it, buddy! Boy did you get it!"

Once the laughter died down, Taylor turned up the radio just a little. One song played and ended, then the first chords of "Jesus Freak" played and Jack immediately reached over and cranked up the sound. Taylor looked over at him, surprised as the young man flawlessly sang every part, rapping in a way that rivaled Mr. Mac himself. Jack was in a world of his own as he sang. It was like Brian had come back to life and was sitting next to him.

Taylor recalled the dream he had about Brian in the car with him and the conversation they had. That was right before he found Jack in the building. Brian's question was answered that night. Yes, Taylor would be willing to risk his life for someone he didn't know if God asked him to do so. He walked through fire to save Jack without giving it a second thought.

By 2:00, they were in Colorado and decided to stop for a late lunch. Jack offered to take the next shift of driving so Taylor could sit back and relax. Taylor took him up on it and reclined the passenger seat.

"Do you know I have never sat in this seat before?" Taylor observed. "I could get used to this." He closed his eyes.

"You should let me pay for every other tank of gas too." Jack suggested.

Taylor opened his left eye and frowned at Jack. "We'll see." He said and closed his eye again.

"Yes we will." Jack said under his breath, which made Taylor laugh.

"Brat." He mumbled. Jack responded by turning the volume up on the radio. It was surprising how quickly the two had eased into their roles – a friendship that was brand new but seemed seasoned and comfortable.

After a few hours, they stopped for gas and a restroom break. They bought drinks and snacks and Taylor took the next shift of driving. He asked Jack to tell him about songwriting and playing music in his youth group. He listened attentively while Jack told him all about his love for music from an early age and how it had evolved throughout the years. He told Taylor about his so-called rock star fantasies where he performed on stage in front of thousands in a huge venue. It made him laugh when he looked back on it now, but during those younger years he had woven an intricate fantasy.

In turn, Taylor shared his "go to" rock star fantasy as a teen. He was on stage sitting at a state of the art drum kit. All around him were bright lights and there were hundreds of people in the audience. Six huge studio cameras followed his every move. As he played, his sticks moved ridiculously fast while his foot was like a piston on the base drum, moving at impossible speeds. This was his moment in the limelight and he was ripping the kit apart. It sounded like two drummers playing at once. Suddenly he stopped, just stopped cold. From beside him came a blast on another kit and he recognized the style immediately. He looked over and saw Buddy Rich. He was dueling it out with Buddy Rich, the greatest drummer to ever swing a stick. Buddy was laying it down and killing over there. Without a doubt, this was the fastest anyone had ever heard Buddy play and it was awesome. He played for about thirty seconds and stopped. It was Taylor's turn again. This time, he was drumming at a blistering speed, faster than anything his mind could comprehend. But it was more than just speed. He was laying down an intricate pattern all the while his sticks not even visible. He glanced at Buddy and saw that his jaw had dropped and his mouth hung open. He shook his head as if in disbelief and Taylor's confidence hit the ceiling. He was out-drumming Buddy Rich! After thirty seconds, he stopped and the crowd screamed with approval. Buddy paused for dramatic effect and then he let it rip. His speed was inhuman and his body language made one thing perfectly clear. This was Buddy Rich using every ounce of drumming expertise in his arsenal. All the decades, all the gigs, all the live performances had culminated in this moment. Buddy was matching Taylor's last solo and then time was up and Buddy stopped. The crowd jumped to their feet. The roar was deafening.

Buddy looked over at Taylor and smiled that Buddy Rich smile. Taylor smiled back, and winked.

"And then what happened?" Jack asked, hoping it didn't stop there.

"Well, I don't think words can describe the way I defied the laws of physics and bested Buddy Rich." Taylor chuckled. "We'll just say when I stopped I was the reigning king of the kit."

"That's a great rock star fantasy, man." Jack grinned with approval. "Are you pretty good on the drums?"

Taylor almost hurt himself laughing so hard. "Uh no." He said flatly when he caught his breath. "I played with some guys in junior high and high school and I auditioned for a few bands. But nothing ever came of it." He thought about the sting of rejection after each audition. "I really wanted to do something great, you know. Something that would make people ask who I was."

"You may get your wish, Taylor." Jack observed. "But it may not be with drumsticks in your hands."

Taylor nodded in agreement. This mission could slip under the radar or it could attract a lot of attention depending on what happened down the road. He told Jack about the dream about driving with Brian and what he had suggested Taylor might be faced with. Jack was beyond the point of being surprised by anything anymore. So when Taylor said the day after that dream was when he found Jack in the burning building, he nodded because it only made sense it would happen that way. Then the topic shifted to Caroline showing up and leading them to the Mill.

"I sense you might have a thing for her." Jack teased and punched Taylor in the arm playfully.

"Too young." Taylor reminded him. "She is interesting though, isn't she? Mysterious." He lifted his eyebrows and waggled them up and down which made Jack laugh.

"Don't ever do that again." Jack insisted which made Taylor laugh.

"What? This?" He did it again. "You mean don't ever do this again?" He repeated the movement.

"You're a decent looking guy but you won't have a chance with any woman if you ever do that in front of anyone." Jack said trying to act serious.

"You're saying you think I have a shot with her?" Taylor joked.

"No way. No chance. At all." Jack replied dryly.

"But you just said I was handsome." Taylor protested.

"I did not say that." Jack remained straight faced. "I said you were decent looking. That's only one step up from Elephant Man."

"You don't know, she might dig that." Taylor winked. "I think I have a shot."

"No one digs that." Jack was smiling now in spite of his attempts to play the straight man in this comedic exchange. "She's weird, I will give you that, but I don't think she's that weird."

"This is shocking and terrible news." Taylor pretended to be crushed. "I may not recover. You are really mean."

Jack burst out laughing and Taylor lost his composure as well. They goofed around like this until it was time to stop for the night. By 8:00 they were ready to call it a day and get dinner and some rest. They checked into a decent looking hotel just off the interstate in Colorado, not too far from the Kansas border. They settled into a room and ordered some pizza and were asleep by 10:30 pm.

CHAPTER 20

Saturday, they each drove in 3 hour shifts until they stopped for the evening in a small Missouri town called Horatio. They located the nicest hotel in town, cleaned up and set out to find a place for dinner that played live music. It was Saturday night after all. Although it seemed like weeks since they had met, this was the first weekend they had known each other. Considering the events of the past week, they were both ready to blow off some steam.

They ended up at a place called The Worm's Nest. Admittedly it was an odd name for an eating establishment but once they got there they understood why the place was called The Worm's Nest. The history of the restaurant was colorfully portrayed with words and pictures in the front foyer/waiting area. While Horatio was a small town, it seemed people came from miles around for the dining and entertainment. Worm was the nickname of the owner whose real name was John Williams. There was no real explanation as to how John got the nickname Worm, but he had been known by that name since he was a teenager growing up in this town. He loved music and was a fellow drummer, much to Taylor's surprise. He had drummed in a small local band when he was young but as an adult he decided to take over and resurrect a dying eating establishment called, Frank's. John, aka Worm funneled generous funds into the place to remodel, revitalize and rejuvenate. He gave local bands from surrounding counties opportunities to play and get experience and exposure. There was evidence via framed news clippings that a few of the bands who were discovered at The Worm's Nest had gone on to have success in larger metropolitan areas and at least one had recorded an album and had a song played on the radio. Tonight, he had a band called Frenzy playing classic 70's tunes, which pleased Taylor.

"Stick with me, kid." Taylor teased. "I'll show you what's up."

"I know my 70's music." Jack laughed. Taylor was about to find out that Jack was very well versed in all music genres from all eras.

They played a good-natured game of 70's music trivia while they waited for their food, battling over who could guess the song name and original artist first as each song started. They were both really good and it resulted in a lot of laughter. They eased off the competitiveness while they ate and simply enjoyed the band. When they were ready to leave the restaurant, their bellies were full and their spirits lifted. It was good for them to be normal guys just out having fun.

On the way out as they were walking passed the bar, Taylor stopped short. Jack took a few steps before he realized Taylor was not with him. He turned to see his friend frozen in place. He rushed to Taylor's side. "What's up, man?"

Taylor inhaled deeply. "Do you smell that?" He asked.

Jack sniffed. "Cigarettes and beer?"

"Roses."

"No." Jack shook his head. "I can't smell it."

"I can." Taylor said. He surveyed the bar and saw a lot of people who he knew could be dismissed immediately. Then one girl caught his eye. "There." He said, nodding towards a young woman at the far end of the bar. She had long wavy blonde hair, styled just so. Her makeup was perfect and she had a sparkle in her eyes. She looked directly at Taylor and held his gaze for a moment before looking away.

"You think?" Jack asked.

"Maybe." He said in a voice that was barely audible above the din in the bar. Then he walked over to the bar and sat down with one seat between them. Jack watched from the sidelines. The girl looked over at Taylor after he sat down and smiled then brushed the hair away from her bare shoulder. She wore a white halter style dress and small pearl earrings. Taylor returned the smile but it conveyed mere politeness and no real interest. Jack marveled at how well his friend handled himself. By the looks of it, Taylor was going to make her instigate a conversation. After a few minutes, she did.

"The band is pretty good." She said, leaning over the seat between her and Taylor.

Taylor nodded politely and flagged the bartender. The look on the girl's face was priceless. Jack had to put his hand over his mouth to stifle a chuckle. She could not believe Taylor was not falling all over himself to make a move on her. She reached into her purse, took out a mirror and lipstick and proceeded to make sure her look was on point. After applying another coat of cherry red lipstick, she was satisfied that it was. She snapped the mirror closed and tucked it and the lipstick away in her purse. Meanwhile the bartender had approached Taylor and took his order, bringing him a small glass with soda and a lime. By all appearances he was drinking hard liquor mixed with coke. Jack knew Taylor was not a drinker so it was undoubtedly plain old soda. Taylor took a drink and made a face as if it were too strong. His eyes met Jack's and he winked. Jack did actually laugh out loud, then looked around to see if anyone had noticed. No one was paying attention to him. He remained where he was, leaning up against the wall near other people waiting to get a table. He blended in perfectly.

"Can I ask you a question?" The girl leaned in towards Taylor again.

"Free country." Taylor said, staring forward. It was obvious that she was off balance. He wasn't staring longingly into her eyes, saying all the right things to try to take her home.

"Do you believe in fate?" She asked. That got his attention.

"No ma'am." He said looking her square in the eyes. "I do not."

Her mouth was open as if she were going to speak but she snapped it shut and gave him a look of confusion. Then a sly smile crept up on her face. Her eyes sparkled brilliant blue. She stood up, smoothed the front of her dress, walked over and stopped behind Taylor's chair. He didn't flinch. She leaned in to whisper in his ear. "I do." She said and raised her other hand and dropped a single long stemmed red rose on the bar in front of him. She turned and disappeared into the crowd behind the bar.

Jack watched this without fully understanding what he was seeing but when she dropped the rose in front of Taylor, his legs lost their ability to hold up the rest of his body. He fell back against the wall and started to go down. Luckily, he righted himself before he hit the floor.

The scent of the rose overwhelmed Taylor when she dropped it in front of him and time seemed to stand still. It was her! He tried to move but couldn't do it fast enough. By the time his body received the message from his brain to turn around and get moving she was already gone. He turned back around in time to see Jack making long strides to get to him where he sat.

"What just happened?" Jack was out of breath. His heart was pounding wildly.

"That was Rose." Taylor said throwing his hands up in defeat. "And I let her slip right through my fingers."

"She'll turn up again." Jack assured him.

Taylor drained his glass, threw a ten-dollar bill down on the bar and stood up. "Let's get out of here."

"Where to, Boss?" Jack asked.

"We drive around." Taylor said. "I have a feeling this night is long from over." They left The Worm's Nest and climbed into the Maxima and headed south.

They had a full tank of gas and it was a good thing because they drove around for well over an hour. If their lives depended on it they could not have backtracked and found their way out of the twisty-turn back roads they had ventured down and doubled back on. Finally, they crossed a narrow wooden bridge with rickety planks and followed the deeply rutted dirt road until it dead ended. Jack looked over at Taylor who was focused but on edge.

"What do you think?" Jack asked as they sat staring at the trees beyond their headlights.

"Let's get some air." Taylor answered. He killed the engine but left the headlights on even though they hardly needed them. The moon was big and full and illuminated the area better than a streetlight. They walked around and stretched their legs.

"None of this makes sense." Taylor said raking his fingers through his hair. Then he turned his head sharply. Jack also heard the sound of sticks breaking beneath someone's feet. All the hair on his arms and neck were standing on end. There was more crunching then a man appeared out of the darkness.

"You fellas lost?" He said, his hands shoved deep in his pockets.

"Just stretching our legs, my friend." Taylor said and gave Jack a warning look.

"I'm not your friend, mister." The stranger said. He appeared to be in his mid-thirties and was tall with very long shiny dark hair. His eyes were menacing as they narrowed their gaze at Jack. "Yours neither." He added as he pulled his right hand out of his pocket and with a click a blade popped up. *Switchblade,* Jack thought. *Great.*

"What's your problem, man?" Jack asked, poised to tackle the guy. Out of the corner of his eye he saw Taylor shake his head no. Jack relaxed and stepped back.

"No problem at all. In fact," The dark stranger said. "I'm thinking I just hit the jackpot. Two wallets and a car. That's a pretty good night from where I stand."

What happened next was a blur. Out of the darkness someone came in what could only be described as stealth mode, silently launched themselves in a sweeping motion and down went the knife-wielding bad guy. He was out cold.

PART 2

CHAPTER 1

"We are probably looking at the second week of December for the release." Kayleigh Thompson peered over her dark rimmed glasses at her client who appeared to be preoccupied with something outside the office window. "Does that work for you, Kate?"

Katherine Abbot turned her attention back to her literary agent after zoning out for a few seconds. "Give me a minute." She picked up her cell phone and opened the calendar. Today was June 7th, so six months exactly. That was plenty of time to get her act together. "Should be fine." She said and turned off her phone.

Kayleigh put her pen down and crossed her arms as she leaned back in her chair. "That means book tours during the holidays, Kate. It's the down side of releasing strategically to reap big holiday sales." She studied her client.

Kate was tall and slender with nice muscle definition in her arms, shoulders, back and legs. There was just enough to create very lovely, feminine curves. She didn't wear much makeup because she simply didn't need it. Her complexion was even and clear. Her blue eyes and thick dark lashes rarely needed dressing up unless she was going out. She kept her eyebrows tweezed and shaped into a classic arch and they were dark enough (in spite of being a blonde) that they did not require filling in. She usually opted for a light pink lip gloss rather than a darker lipstick. Kate's blonde hair went passed her shoulders and was mostly one length with the exception of a few longer layers around her face. She didn't have to fuss much with her hair for it to look as if she had put effort into it but often just threw it up in a loose chignon or ponytail. Today was no exception. She was dressed very casually for her visit to Kayleigh's office in yoga pants and a loose-fitting tee shirt, hair pulled back in a low ponytail.

"I don't have much in the way of family, Kayleigh. You know that. Just my grandmother and I feel pretty confident I can manage a day or two to see her around Christmas." Kate shifted in her chair. More than anything she wanted out of the office before Kayleigh asked the question that she desperately wanted to avoid.

"Well, I know he's not technically family but won't Seth be affected if you are on a book tour during the holidays?" And there it was, right on cue. Kate bristled at the sound of his name.

"About Seth." Kate took a deep breath and tried to smile. Her attempt failed and what Kayleigh saw looked more like someone with brain freeze, conveying acute discomfort, possibly pain. "We broke up."

"I didn't mean to pry, Kate." Kayleigh put her hands up apologetically.

"No big deal." Kate lied.

"I've known you for 8 years. You know you can talk to me if you need a shoulder, right?" Kayleigh offered.

"Of course." The truth was Kate did need a shoulder but she never knew how to reach out to people when she was in pain. "Maybe drinks one night this week?"

"I'm free tonight." Kayleigh said. She looked at her watch. It was 5:18 pm. "In fact, you're my last appointment. If you're not busy, why don't we just go from here and hit happy hour at Barney's down the street. My treat."

"My social calendar is ridiculously wide open." Kate replied.

Kayleigh shut down her computer and grabbed her bag. Kate followed her out. "I'm heading home, Susan. Have a good evening." Kayleigh said to her secretary as she locked her office door. Susan waved and said good night in return. The two ladies made their way to the elevator in silence. Kate's mind was frantically searching for how to begin the dark tale that was the end of her and Seth.

By the time they got to Barney's Kate had come to the conclusion that she was making a mountain out of a molehill. So the story was embarrassing – big deal! They found a place in the back corner and settled in. Kayleigh ordered a glass of pinot noir and Kate decided on chardonnay.

"When did all this happen, Kate?" Kayleigh asked, more than a little worried about her client/friend.

"About six months ago." Kate answered. The look of shock on Kayleigh's face made Kate feel like a jerk for being so secretive. "I've been laying low since it happened, so don't feel bad for not noticing. I haven't felt very, um – social."

"Okay so start at the beginning because the last time I saw the two of you, I would have sworn I could hear wedding bells ringing." Kayleigh shook her head sadly.

"Well you saw us together at the party you threw for me after "Losers Weepers" made the bestsellers list, right?" Kate asked and Kayleigh nodded yes.

"Things were really good for another 6 months I guess. Then he got a new assistant at work. He started working longer hours and staying out later at night. The more his professional life flourished the more his home life died on the vine. I noticed after

161

the first month of hearing all about this great assistant that he didn't touch me as often when he walked passed me or sit up close to me on the couch. After a year and a half together, suddenly his physical patterns started changing. After 3 months he had stopped saying 'I love you', except as a response when I said it first. He had always been the one to say it first." Kate's eyes were filling up with tears. Kayleigh slid a napkin over to her. She took a minute then continued. "I kept asking him what was wrong and what I needed to do to make things right. He insisted everything was fine, the same as always. But I knew it was a lie and too many late nights had me suspicious. Then one night he woke up around 4 am and got out of bed, walked over to his dresser where his phone was. I watched him check his phone and then take it and leave the room." Kate recalled. Kayleigh sat across from her with her mouth agape. "The next morning while he was in the shower I did something I never thought I would do. I went through his phone and read the texts between him and Jessica, the assistant." She remembered how the whole thing had left her feeling queasy. "I won't go into the gory details, but it left nothing to the imagination. I felt betrayed."

"Oh my goodness! What did you do?" Kayleigh was leaning forward, eyes wide with disbelief.

"I put the phone back and let him go to work." Kate smiled and took a sip of her chardonnay.

"And?" Kayleigh prompted. "You did NOT just let this go. I know you better than that."

"And then I called a couple of friends and I emptied the house in less than 4 hours." Kate grinned sheepishly.

"Okay." Kayleigh nodded. "That sounds like the old Kate, right there."

"I only took what was mine, but really almost everything

was mine. I left a pillow and a blanket for him on the floor of the bedroom. I mean, I'm not a total jerk." She smirked. Then her expression sobered considerably. "Two days later I realized I had left something behind that I really needed. I went to the house and his car was there in the middle of the day along with another car I didn't recognize."

Kayleigh narrowed her eyes. "You must be kidding. Is he really that stupid?"

"I'm not and yes, he is." Kate advised. "He had Jessica there in 'our' house the moment he found out I was gone. He had moved her in, Kayleigh. Two days. I guess we never really know what people are capable of. On the upside, I got in shape and have become fairly skilled at kickboxing. I actually started taking classes when he stopped touching me. I needed an outlet for my frustrations." She flexed her arm and watched Kayleigh's eyes widen. "I also started lifting after I left him. I've put on some muscle. No one is ever going to hurt me again."

"Is there more to this story than just a cheating boyfriend?" Kayleigh was suspicious of that last remark.

"Maybe." Kate peered down into her wine glass. "I don't even know why I was upset when I caught him cheating." Kate murmured. "It wasn't the best relationship anyway."

"Well, I'm not defending him, but few relationships are perfect." Kayleigh reasoned.

"Especially when you're with someone who likes to knock you around." Kate said softly. She remembered the countless times when he had been drunk and had hit her. The times he had pushed her down and kicked her. The times he had pushed her out of bed when she was asleep and demanded she sleep on the floor like a dog. The dirty secret she had kept for so long was out and it was still just as repulsive in the light of day as it had been hidden in the shadows. The shame was crippling. How do you tell someone you went through that and did nothing about it? But there was no longer a reason to keep quiet about it. So she told Kayleigh about all the ways Seth had degraded and humiliated her as well as the acts of physical abuse.

Sitting across from her, Kayleigh teared up as she heard every awful detail. How she wished she had known and could have saved Kate from some of that pain– any of it. But Kate was too proud to ask for help or to admit she was a victim.

"I'm not going to make excuses." Kate said finally. "I stayed because I didn't want to be a quitter. I had given up on so many other relationships. I just thought I needed to be tougher and give him a chance to change. I tried to be better so he would want to change. All he wanted to change was roommates." She shrugged.

A plate of appetizers arrived and they decided to move on to other topics while they enjoyed their food.

"So, what's next for Kate Abbot?" Kayleigh asked pointing at Kate with a buffalo wing then making a clucking sound.

Kate laughed. "I'm going to take some time off and go home and visit my grandmother."

"As your friend, I am really glad to hear that." Kayleigh took a bite and paused while she chewed." As your agent I have to ask about the next book."

"Don't worry, Boss. I will not fall short of my contractual obligations." Kate did air quotes. "But you should know the next book is already in the bag." She smiled broadly, obviously very pleased with herself. "I had a LOT of time on my hands. Six months with literally no distractions outside of fitness related activities." Kate explained. I hammered it out with very little effort. It's kind of dark though. Hopefully you will approve."

Kayleigh chuckled. "You're my favorite writer, Kate. I'd pay to read your grocery list."

"You may want to reserve such bold statements until after you have read the manuscript." Kate advised.

"Okay, I can do that." Kayleigh agreed. "Do I get it before you leave to visit Grandma?"

"Sure, why not?" Kate didn't really want to leave it sitting in her apartment anyway. "I can drop it off before I leave on Thursday. I'll email you the digital file if you are still interested after you read it."

"Sounds good. How long will you be gone?"

"I'm leaving it open ended, actually." Kate had decided she needed an undetermined period away from San Francisco to decide what was next in her life.

"I see." Kayleigh understood that Kate needed time away to get her groove back. Having no restrictions or timelines would certainly be liberating for her. "I hope you will keep in touch with me though."

"Of course, I will." Kate promised. "I have someone apartment sitting for me so I don't have to worry about the place being empty while I'm gone. She's going to water my plants, handle my mail, stuff like that."

"So, are you flying out or driving?"

"I'm driving. I love the windshield time to think and mull things over. Who knows, I might come up with some great book ideas between here and there."

Kayleigh laughed, knowing that this was a very plausible outcome. "Just be careful. You've got a temper and it looks like now you are some kind of lethal weapon with that body of yours."

That made Kate laugh. It was true, she had been known to have some road rage moments in her life but the thought of stopping her car and jumping out to kick-box another driver into submission was pretty funny. Kate had turned her body into a strong and efficient weapon. One that would ensure she was never victimized again physically. As far as emotionally, well she had that covered too. She had spent the last six months erecting walls around her heart. Outside those walls was a moat filled with sharks and alligators and piranha. Snipers were perched on the tops of the walls as backup for the moat of doom. The exaggerated imagery came easily for her but in truth she had indeed hardened her heart and no one was getting through again unless a miracle took place. She didn't put any stock in those kinds of things anyway. Miracles were strictly for movies and books.

Kayleigh sat across from her friend, knowing her well enough to see that she was lost in her own thoughts. Kate was a brilliant woman. She had always been warm and friendly but it was not easy to get close to her. Kayleigh had known Kate for 8 years and had been her agent for the past 6 years. They were friends before Kate decided to make a career of writing and with Kayleigh's occupation, it was only logical that they join forces when she wrote her first novel. Over the years Kayleigh had watched Kate go from a very open and outgoing person always surrounded by a group of friends to the wounded and isolated woman who sat across from her now. A succession of bad relationships had slowly chipped away at that carefree young woman. Now at 32 years of age with the baggage of bad decisions and heartbreaks heaped on her, she seemed defeated. The Kate she looked at today was a far cry from the one she met at the age of 24.

She could feel the absence of joy in Kate and it was hard to accept. She knew Kate was a stranger to the concepts of faith and the grace of God and while she couldn't ask her friend to pray, she could pray FOR her. Kayleigh closed her eyes and asked God to be with her friend and help her find her way. Help her find comfort in Him and help her be open to love again someday.

"I can only promise I will try not to break anyone in a fit of rage." Kate conceded. "Honestly, I expect a quiet, uneventful road trip to the east coast where I will end up in my favorite little town baking cookies with my grandmother and walking along the beach."

Soon the topic of work came back around as it always had a tendency to do. Before they left the restaurant and went to their respective homes, Kate promised again that she would deliver the manuscript before she left on her road trip/vacation. Kayleigh seemed satisfied enough with that and was looking forward to reading Kate's "latest and greatest" as soon as it was in her hot little hands.

The next day Kate took her Honda Accord in for the usual maintenance for fluids, filters, belts and oil change. An hour later she left the automotive place with a clean bill of health and a feeling of confidence that she and "Honcho" would make it across country just fine.

She packed clothes and a few toiletries and moved on to the other essentials for travel. She grabbed a novel from the book shelf and set it on the table with her laptop, tablet, power cords, chargers and headphones. She stood looking at the items, hands on her hips knowing she was forgetting something. Manuscript! Kayleigh would have had her head on a platter if she had left without dropping it off. She grabbed it from her desk and added it to the pile. That would sit on the seat next to her to remind her to stop by

167

the office and hand it over on the way out of town. When she felt she had addressed everything on her checklist, she had some dinner and relaxed for the evening, feeling excited about seeing her grandmother again.

After she dropped off the manuscript and said goodbye to Kayleigh the next day, she turned on navigation and typed in her destination. She headed towards I-80 as directed and followed Honcho's every command along the way. As she drove through California into Nevada, Kate thought about her grandmother and her childhood.

Katherine Layla Abbot was born on April 24, 1984 in Chelsea, Massachusetts. Her mother, Gina was 15 when she gave birth. The baby's father was one of several possible candidates, none of which wanted anything to do with mother or baby. Gina's mother, Barbara stepped up and took care of the infant so Gina could finish high school and graduate. Because Barbara was able to take the baby with her to her office, the two were inseparable and by the time Kate was a toddler, she thought of Barbara as her mother and Gina as a sister. Barbara took care of all baby Kate's needs while Gina lived out the life of a typical teenage girl in the 80's. By the time she graduated from high school, Gina was ready to start a new life elsewhere. When Kate was three years old, Gina disappeared forever and never bothered to check back in again.

Barbara worked hard to make sure Kate had everything she needed. There were not a lot of extras but she covered the essentials and Kate never felt deprived. She was involved in Kate's school life as much if not more than many biological parents.

In spite of a happy childhood and normal upbringing, as a young woman Kate hungered for love. And not just any kind of love. She longed for perfect love. She spent her teenage years creating elaborate fantasies in which she conjured up the perfect mate. He was strong yet compassionate. Kind but logical. He was selfless and giving, always doing for others and putting her up on a pedestal. He was brave enough to fight any adversary who might wish to harm her but forgiving and gentle with those in need. He was romantic and a poet. His words would make her heart soar, testifying to love that could conquer anything and everything. He knew her every thought and anticipated her needs before she knew them herself. His sense of humor complemented her own and he made her laugh every day that they were together. This was the man she created – the standard to which she held all young men to in her teens and later as an adult. It would seem she had doomed herself to failure and disappointment by design. No one could stack up against an ideal partner like that. So, it was no surprise that Kate's romantic life was one disaster after another. She always had such high hopes at first only to be disappointed time after time. It never even occurred to her that she had set the bar so impossibly high that no one could hope to measure up. She felt certain that if she persevered she would find her soul mate. Unfortunately, some possessed a few of the characteristics she required (or they pretended to) but then their very unpleasant sometimes nasty qualities would surface and she would end the relationship and move on to the next. This was the ebb and flow of her love life.

Having just turned 32 years old in April, Kate had finally sworn off love forever. She had experienced enough disappointment for a woman twice her age and she had officially had enough. Friends and acquaintances were fine but no more romance and definitely no more love. If she felt the need for a companion later in life she'd find herself a cocker spaniel and call it a day.

It was after midnight when she finally decided to stop for the night just outside Salt Lake City. She didn't bother getting anything to eat even though she was starving but instead checked into a hotel and was asleep the moment her head hit the pillow. As a rule, she fell asleep with ease and enjoyed undisturbed, dreamless sleep until she woke the next morning. Such was not the case this time. Although she had fallen asleep right away from sheer exhaustion, she now found herself in a very vivid dream.

In this dream, she sat outdoors with a dozen or more people in the dark around a campfire. Everyone was talking as fish cooked over the flames on a strange looking pan. The smell was amazing. She was so hungry and she felt like she hadn't eaten for days. She put her hand over her tummy as it rumbled. Someone chuckled and nudged her and she laughed. The person on the other side of her handed her a piece of bread and a few olives and dates. She took it all happily and said thank you. She couldn't wait to dig into that fish though. Her surroundings felt familiar and welcoming. She was comfortable with these people although she couldn't say exactly who they were. They were friends, she did know that much. She herself felt very different, like someone who had never been hurt by anyone before. It was a liberating feeling. She felt like someone who lived moment by moment with no expectations and no baggage. She ate her food slowly, relishing every delicious bite and began to feel drowsy. Someone told her not to fall asleep before he came. She nodded but then lay down with her head on her arm. She watched the flames flicker in the darkness and her eyes became heavy. Someone shouted excitedly that he was coming. She wanted to rise but her body was so weary and her satisfied tummy had set the stage for sleep. She drifted. She was faintly aware of celebration around her then a presence nearby that was magnetic. She willed her eyes to open but they refused. He's coming... echoed in her mind

over and over. A gentle touch to her forehead then a
whisper, "Rest well, Beloved." And she was swept away
into nothingness.

She sat up in bed with a gasp, wide awake, disoriented and confused. She looked around for a clock. 2:12 am. She flung herself back down on the mattress. She didn't know what to make of the dream. It had seemed so real that she could still smell the succulent aroma of the fish that was being grilled over the fire, not to mention the sense of peace she felt when someone touched her forehead. Who was "he"? The one she and everyone else was all up in arms about? Was he the one who touched her? How could she fall asleep when she was so excited about him coming? And since when did she go camping? The dream made no sense. Having had little experience with dreams, she felt like it begged to be decoded. Finally, she gave up and went back to sleep. There were no more dreams and she didn't stir until she woke up the next morning when the alarm sounded.

The next day she drove through Salt Lake City and was in Cheyenne, Wyoming 8 hours later where she found a hotel for the night. By 10:30 am Saturday morning she was ready to hit the road. As she drove, she was so preoccupied with ideas for a budding new novel that she didn't even notice when the nav took her south into Kansas instead of continuing east into Iowa and Illinois, the logical path of least resistance to Massachusetts. She found herself rolling into a small town near Kansas City, Missouri around 6pm. It really wasn't that big of a deal to be diverted and she could simply re-set nav in the morning. She found a decent looking hotel and checked in for the night. After asking a couple of members of the hotel staff, she decided to check out a local bar and grill for dinner. The place doing a booming business on a Saturday night for such a small town. She had a moderate wait before she was shown to a table. By 9:30 pm she was paying the check and leaving the restaurant. She walked to her car and reached out for the door when she noticed it wasn't her car.

She looked around, confused. This was where she parked, she remembered it clearly because it was right in front of the neon "Open" sign in the window. She hit the remote and waited for the bark of the horn. Nothing. Panic set in and she started scouring the parking lot for her car. It was gone. She went back inside and asked for the manager. Apparently, this wasn't the first time a patron's car had been boosted while they were eating there. She felt herself about to fly into a rage but stopped before she made the situation worse. She took her cell phone out of her purse and called the police. They came and took her statement and she made her official report. The local police seemed confident it was probably just kids messing around and her car would turn up somewhere in the morning. They left and she decided to walk off her anger. She estimated she was approximately 5 miles from the hotel which was not a bad thing. She would be calm by the time she got there and she would be tired. The restaurant was in a rural area so she felt safe keeping off the road and out of sight. She had a good sense of the direction of her hotel and set out on foot.

The amount of traffic that was on the road she planned on taking back to the hotel was too heavy for her comfort. She pulled out her phone and accessed a county map online. Taking back roads would be shorter and would lead her ultimately to her hotel unseen by drivers. Perhaps that would be the prudent choice for a woman alone walking in the dark in a strange place. She ducked through the trees down a narrow dirt road. The full moon lent ample light for her to see everything around her. She walked with ease for about an hour when she noticed the headlights of a parked car just beyond a bridge up ahead. She really didn't want to encounter anyone out in the woods at night but that was exactly where she needed to cut through on another smaller road that led to the hotel. It was probably just teenagers making out. Certain she could slip passed them, she crept quietly across the bridge. By the time she reached the end she could see that the road ahead dead ended. She was wrong about it being teenagers. Three men stood by the car, two with their backs to the car and one guy facing them holding something up. The two men near the car looked worried.

She sighed. *Walk away, Kate.* She told herself. But her legs kept moving and she crouched down as she moved in slowly for a closer look. Now it was clear that the one guy was holding a knife. Well now she had to get involved, didn't she? It didn't take long to see that the guy with the knife meant to rob the other two and take their car and possibly do something worse to them. *Sorry. Not tonight, pal.* She said under her breath. Without making a sound she launched herself at him from the side and placed a perfect roundhouse kick to the side of the bad guy's head. He went down like a ton of bricks. The knife flew from his hand and landed in the dirt. She kicked it into the brush while the other two men stared at her dumbfounded.

CHAPTER 2

Jack and Taylor looked at each other, hardly able to believe what just happened.

"What?" The woman who saved them looked at them and blinked. "You weren't expecting me?" She asked. She was a pretty blonde who was built like a warrior. Jack's mouth refused to work. Fortunately, Taylor's was still functioning properly.

"Just wondering what took you so long?" Taylor sounded calm but his eyes revealed his surprise.

"Right." The girl said with a deadpan expression. "I'm Kate. You too have names or am I supposed to guess?" Jack narrowed his eyes at her. She wasn't exactly pleasant, even if she was beautiful and had just saved the day.

"You have a problem, pretty boy?" She challenged him.

"Good grief." Jack sighed. "I would almost rather deal with the thug with the knife." He said.

Kate glared at him. "I can always wake him up. Or would you like to get over yourself and help me tie him up?" She addressed Jack. He crossed arms over his chest defiantly and leaned on the Maxima.

"I have some rope in the trunk." Taylor said and moved quickly to the back of the car.

"At least half this duo has his head screwed on straight." Kate taunted Jack.

"Who do you think you are?" Jack took a step towards her, really ticked off now.

"I dunno." She held her arms out in a V. "Maybe just the chick that saved your –"

"Got the rope!" Taylor interrupted and held up the loop of yellow nylon rope.

"Let's tie him to that tree over there." Kate pointed to the left. "You can call the cops to pick him up later or not. It's your deal, dude."

"I'm Taylor, by the way." He put his hand out. "I'm really happy to meet you, Kate." He went down on one knee, rolled the thug over and pulled his wallet from his back pocket. His driver's license said his name was Victor Taro. Taylor stuffed the wallet back in the man's pocket. "That's my buddy, Jack." He nodded towards Jack who remained several feet away with a scowl on his face.

"So, Jack." Kate said. "You going to let your boyfriend do all the work or are you going to lend a hand?" Jack gritted his teeth and moved in to help Taylor drag Taro over to a tree and tie him up.

"She's a piece of work." Jack muttered under his breath to Taylor.

Taylor chuckled. "She is a live wire, no doubt." He said. "But she literally saved us, Jack."

"I think I would rather have been robbed." Jack said.

"I heard that." Kate said from several feet away. "Don't fall all over yourself with gratitude, Blondie. You might pull a muscle."

Jack never thought he could dislike anyone as much and as quickly as he disliked her. But after he thought about it he agreed with Taylor. She did save them and it wouldn't kill him to be civil.

"Let's start over, shall we?" Jack asked, walking up to her and giving her his most charming smile. "Thank you, Kate for saving us. What can we do for you to show our gratitude?" He took her hand and kissed it. Kate's first reaction was to slug the jerk for presuming he had the right to touch her. But then she checked her ego and decided she could to try to be nice. After all, even though his gender had tried to break her, this man in particular had done nothing to her at all.

"No thanks necessary." She pulled her hand away. "I just happened to be…"

"…in the neighborhood." Both Taylor and Jack finished for her. They all laughed in spite of the awkwardness of the situation. It seemed to help thaw the iceberg that surrounded Kate.

"Seriously, I'm sorry if I came off as ungrateful. "Jack said. His blue eyes bore into hers. She couldn't help but accept his apology which seemed sincere. But she warned herself to be careful. He looked exactly like the type of guy that always got her into trouble in the past. *Be gracious and move on*, she told herself.

"Don't worry about it." Kate said. She would never see them again anyway so she could play nice for the short time she had to endure Blondie.

"That was amazing, Kate." Taylor beamed at her. Now this one she liked. He seemed very genuine. Transparent even. He had zero issues. He was definitely a good guy.

"Anyone would have done the same." She shrugged.

"Yeah, if they were a ninja maybe." Taylor laughed. Kate smiled in spite of herself.

"What can I say? Sometimes a woman's skills can come in handy." She smiled at him and started to walk away.

"We owe you, Kate." He said. "Can we give you a ride somewhere? You shouldn't be wandering around alone out here."

"I can take care of myself." She turned and gave him a serious look. "Remember who saved who?"

"Jack promises to be nice, don't you Jack?" Taylor elbowed him.

"Yeah, sure!" Jack agreed sweetly. She didn't trust that he could control his disagreeable nature but she was tired and a ride wouldn't be the worst thing in the world if Pretty Boy could manage to stuff a sock in it.

"Alright." Kate headed towards Taylor's car. "Tell the little nymph in the backseat to move over."

"What nymph?" Jack asked running over to the car. About that time Caroline's face appeared in the backseat passenger window. She was smiling and then she put her mouth on the window and blew her cheeks out wide like a puffer fish. Her mouth made a huge O on the window.

"How…?" Taylor started to ask how she'd gotten in the car. Apparently, Kate thought she was with them and had been the entire time. Of course, he and Jack knew better. Seriously, how in the world had she shown up out here?

"Look, I don't want to intrude." Kate raised her hands in surrender.

"Hi ya', Toots." Caroline stepped out of the car. "What's shakin'?"

Kate rolled her eyes. "Are *all* of you from Mayberry?" She shook her head.

"She's cute." Caroline said, looking at Jack.

"Why are you looking at me? She's not mine." Jack was defensive.

"Yet." Caroline winked. "Hey, I'm hungry! Let's get something to eat." She hopped back into the car without closing the door. She leaned out of the door and pointed at Kate. "There's a pancake place next to her hotel."

"There is." Kate slid into the backseat next to Caroline. She wondered how this girl knew she was staying in a hotel, much less which hotel, but she didn't really want to engage in a Q&A so she let it go.

Taylor and Jack exchanged a look. "Let's go get pancakes, I guess." Jack said and climbed into the car.

"I'm Caroline by the way!" She said to Kate.

Chipper much? Kate thought and wished she possessed the power of teleportation. "Kate." She replied.

"I know."

"Oh yeah?" Kate raised her brow.

"I heard you tell the boys." Caroline said. Then she turned her attention to the driver and directed Taylor out of the remote area and back onto the main road to the Pancake House. He really wanted to know how she knew the area, not to mention how she had found them, but he decided discretion was in order. They didn't know Kate and it wouldn't be polite to start firing questions at Caroline in front of her. It was Caroline who made the 911 call from a pay phone at a gas station on the way to let the police know where Taro was tied up. A brief description of what he had done and the location of the knife with his prints on it was some additional information she threw in for good measure.

They pulled up to the Pancake House and Caroline was out of the car almost before it stopped. She sprinted inside and had a big round booth waiting for them by the time they came inside. She was in the middle of the booth. Kate slid in next to her on the left as did Taylor on the right. Jack sat next to Kate.

"Pancakes!" Caroline squealed happily and clapped her hands.

Kate leaned over and whispered to Jack, "Is she on meds?"

Jack laughed and shook his head no. The observation was funny. He looked over at Caroline who was smiling at him expectantly. She reminded him of an excited puppy. Caroline was different and definitely special but she was also crafty, cunning and very sharp. Evelyn, their waitress, came with water and menus. She had 4 coffee mugs, a pot of coffee and cream on her tray as well. They all said yes to coffee. It was after midnight but getting to sleep didn't seem to be a real concern for anyone at this point. They studied their menus and ordered when Evelyn returned.

"So, Kate, what in the world were you doing out there on that road?" Taylor couldn't contain his curiosity any longer.

"Walking to my hotel." She explained. "Someone stole my car while I was having dinner at a restaurant a few miles away." She poured sugar and cream into her coffee and stirred it as she spoke. "I took a shortcut to stay out of sight and off the main road."

"Any idea who took your car?" Jack asked.

"No." She sighed. "I made a police report and Barney Fife told me it was probably just kids out for a joyride. Maybe it will show up tomorrow." She shrugged.

"Another Mayberry reference," Taylor chuckled. Kate looked at him and winked.

179

She was hard to get a bead on, Taylor observed. She kept people at a distance. Maybe it took time for her to warm up to strangers. Not that it mattered. She had saved them and they owed her. End of story.

"Do you think that guy with the knife is part of the other things that have been happening?" Jack asked Taylor.

"I think so, yes." Taylor told him. He looked at Kate whose expression showed she had little interest in their conversation. Caroline on the other hand was listening and extremely interested. She had her elbows on the table and her chin in her hands as her head swiveled back and forth between Jack and Taylor as each spoke.

"Where are you from Kate?" Caroline asked finally.

"San Francisco." Kate answered. "You?"

"Oh you know," Caroline lifted her mug to her mouth and took a sip. "Nowhere. Everywhere. I move around constantly."

"I see." Kate said. "And you two?" She looked at Jack then Taylor. "Are you also gypsies like Tinkerbell over here?" Caroline brightened when she heard the nickname and giggled. Kate rolled her eyes.

"I'm from California, too. Seaside. Just taking a much needed vacation." Taylor answered.

Jack spoke up. "Same here, but I'm heading from LA to Boston to start a new job."

Kate perked up a little bit. "Really? What's the job?"

"Mass General. Burn and Trauma Unit." He noticed her expression brighten when he mentioned Boston. "You like Boston, I take it."

"Grew up there." Kate explained. "Well, just outside Boston in Winthrop. It's a small place you never heard of probably."

Jack laughed. "Small world. I actually do know Winthrop. Point Shirley? Deer Island? The Art Wall? Crest Ave Pizza? The Center?"

Kate was stunned. Really small world. "Okay. Okay." She nodded. "When were you in Winthrop?"

"First time I was 14. My uncle lived there. I spent time there, Salem, Winter Island and of course Boston proper. It was a whirlwind historical tour but I fell in love with the area." He looked over at Taylor and Caroline who both had their heads slightly cocked to the side as they watched the exchange between him and Kate. "That's why I took the job out there when it was offered."

"So you are a doctor?" Kate asked.

"Biomedical Engineer." Jack answered.

"Wow." Kate was impressed.

"What do you do, Kate?" Taylor spoke up.

"I'm a writer." She said.

"No kidding?" Taylor was surprised. He would have pegged her for an attorney or an accountant. "What's your genre?"

"Fiction." She told him. "Suspense."

"You should try romance sometime." Caroline interjected.

"I won't write romance, dear." Kate smirked at her.

"I didn't say write, I said try." Caroline winked and looked at Jack.

"Oh boy." Jack said under his breath. "Caroline, give it up."

"You're smart, Jack but I'm smarter about some things." Caroline said. Then she started bouncing up and down as Evelyn approached with pancakes. The others were eating light but Caroline had ordered a huge stack of blueberry pancakes.

"Syrup, Miss?" Evelyn asked showing her six different types she had on her tray.

"All of them please!" Caroline said excitedly. Evelyn put all six containers on the table and refilled all the coffee mugs. Caroline hummed as she lifted each of the pancakes one by one starting at the bottom and smothered them in different kinds of syrups. Everyone at the table watched, transfixed.

"How is it that someone so tiny can eat that much food?" Jack asked.

"I have a super-fast metabolism, Jack." Caroline told him and shoveled a huge fork full of pancake dripping with syrup into her mouth. She grinned as she chewed and continued humming.

Taylor watched her for a moment then closed his eyes and bowed his head. Jack did the same. Kate watched them with a raised eyebrow. She looked at Caroline who was happily devouring her pancakes and smiling at Kate. "They're praying." She said to Kate through a mouthful of food.

"Why?" Kate whispered.

Caroline laughed. "Why not?"

Taylor and Jack both lifted their heads and opened their eyes and started eating. Taylor had crepes and Jack had a Belgian waffle. Kate had ordered an egg white omelet.

"Where are you headed, Kate?" Caroline asked.

"I was on my way to visit my grandmother in Winthrop." She got a forkful of omelet and blew on it to cool it off.

"How about that?" Caroline grinned at Jack.

He mouthed "stop" to her. She giggled and shook her head no.

Taylor watched and was extremely amused by the entire scene. My how the dynamic had changed with the addition of these two ladies. The air around them crackled with energy. He felt certain that was Caroline's doing. But there was something about Kate. She was compelling. She didn't volunteer anything but she also didn't seem to be pretending to be something other than what they could see.

"Alright Taylor." Caroline looked his way and smiled. "Your turn. What's your line of work?"

"Nothing as impressive as Jack or Kate I'm afraid." He sighed. "I'm a run of the mill Landscape Architect. Boring stuff really." That made Jack laugh because Taylor's profession did not define what he is currently doing with his life. And *that* is far more exciting than what anyone in the room was doing.

"I disagree." Kate said. "I think it would be a fun job. Besides you have to be intelligent and creative in that profession." Taylor hadn't thought about it like that.

"Well that's very kind of you to say." Taylor thanked her.

"So are you three traveling together?" Kate asked.

"No." Jack said. Caroline narrowed her eyes at him.

"Jack and I are traveling east together." Taylor explained. "Caroline here kind of comes and goes as she pleases." He looked at her with a raised eyebrow. She puckered her lips and made a kissing gesture.

Kate was confused but didn't care to dig any deeper. She was tired and her brain was on overload from the events of the night. She had absorbed about as much as she could.

"Taylor and Jack are doing important work for The Kingdom. I just pop in from time to time to lend a hand." Caroline interjected nonchalantly and took another huge forkful of pancake. Jack and Taylor both stopped what they were doing and looked at her wide-eyed. You could have heard a pin drop at that table.

"Excuse me?" Kate asked. "What in the world does that mean?" All eyes were on Caroline.

"The Kingdom?" She pointed upward and grinned. "You know. Of God?"

"Okay." Kate said, putting her napkin in her plate. She was clearly very uncomfortable.

"Kate doesn't believe she has any need for God." Caroline said to Jack. Then she turned to Taylor and said, "Fortunately, The Lord doesn't feel the same way about her." Taylor and Jack were still struck completely speechless by what was happening.

"So, what if I never jumped on the God bandwagon?" Kate defiantly squared off with Caroline. Her voice had a hard edge. "My life has been just fine without that stuff." She didn't like the way Caroline was smirking at her.

"Oh really?" Caroline narrowed her eyes at Kate and the smirk was gone. "You sure about that?"

Suddenly Kate wasn't looking at Caroline anymore. Instead she was watching disturbing scenes from her life. There were so many that flashed before her but she was hit hardest by a couple in particular. She watched herself pursuing a married man, knowing her involvement with him could destroy his family but she didn't care. She only cared about what she wanted. The casualties were of no concern to her. But now she was seeing the devastation she left in her wake. The broken hearts of his small children and the wife who was emotionally destroyed by his betrayal. She watched herself plan and execute an act of revenge upon someone who had wronged her, knowing it would cost the woman her job and probably everything else she had. Now all of the sudden she was privy to the aftermath of her revenge. The cost to the woman was far greater than the wrong she had committed against Kate. In the end depression swallowed up her life and she died alone and broken. The onslaught of guilt and shame was paralyzing. When the room came back into focus she was looking at Caroline, who clearly had something to do with the vision. Her smug expression validated it. It took Kate a moment to compose herself but when she did, she was embarrassed and angry.

"I don't need to justify my life to you or anyone else." She said to them. "I'm never going to see you again after this, and I really don't care what you think of me. So if you'll excuse me, I need to visit the ladies room." She motioned for Jack to let her out. He slid out and let Kate pass.

"Aw, she thinks she has some control over things." Caroline was watching Kate walk away then turned to Taylor. "How cute is that?"

"Who *are* you?" Taylor's face revealed his confusion. "Seriously?"

"Not only who, but where did you come from and how did you find us out there in the middle of nowhere?" Jack interjected.

"I'm not answering any questions until I get more syrup." Caroline licked her fingers. She still had a quarter of her stack but had used all syrup and apparently needed more before she could

185

finish.

"What did you do to Kate?" Jack gave her a stern look. "Her eyes glazed over for a while and she was shaking."

"She needed to see that her statement was untrue." Caroline waved at Evelyn. "More syrup, dear!" She shouted. Evelyn nodded. "The truth is, her life has been anything but *fine without that stuff.*"

"What stuff?" Jack pressed.

"God stuff." Caroline said, her eyes sparkling. "But in her defense, it's not her fault. Her exposure has been very limited and what little she has seen hasn't impressed her. It's why she isn't comfortable around people of faith."

"She doesn't need to be comfortable around us." Jack said. "She helped us, we thanked her and gave her a ride and some food and that's the end of it. She goes her way and we go ours."

"Yeah... about that." Caroline paused while Evelyn put six more containers of syrup on the table and took the empties. "Gracias, Senora!" Evelyn smiled and replied in Spanish.

"What?" It was Taylor who wanted an explanation.

"Well, Taylor." Caroline gave him a serious look. "She didn't find you by accident same as you didn't find Jack by accident." She began saturating her remaining pancakes in various types of syrup. Her eyes danced as she poured.

"How do you know this?" Taylor leaned in towards her.

"I know stuff." She said matter-of-factly. "Like how to find you boys in the Middle of Nowhere Missouri."

"You still haven't explained that." Jack pointed at her.

"I just did, Jack." She said and turned her attention back to her pancakes.

"Thanks for the ride gentlemen." Kate said and tossed a twenty-dollar bill on the table. "Good luck in your travels, Taylor and with your new job, Jack." She turned to walk away.

"Bye Kate!" Caroline called out sweetly. "See you tomorrow!" Kate spun around and started to say something hateful but decided to leave it alone. Instead she gave the girl an obviously fake smile and walked away.

CHAPTER 3

Kate walked across the parking lot to her hotel. Her hands were still shaking as she fumbled for the key to open her room. Teen Witch had put a serious whammy on her, which opened a huge can of worms she didn't even want to deal with. In Kate's world, the supernatural was strictly fiction, but there was no disputing what had happened back there. Ugly highlights (or lowest of lowlights) of her life were crammed down her throat with bonus features of the aftermath of a couple of her particularly bad choices. Caroline had called her out and then showed her to be a liar. Her life hadn't been just fine. She didn't need anyone to tell her that though. Kate was keenly aware of her bad choices, wrong-doings and dirty deeds. She wasn't proud of them by any means but she was human after all and mistakes come with the territory. She failed to see how being a Bible Thumper would have prevented any of that. She thought about it and then realized that was wrong. A Bible Thumper probably wouldn't have had an affair with a married man just for kicks. A Bible Thumper probably wouldn't have destroyed someone for the sake of revenge. But then again, you never know. Some of those people claim to be righteous but are really far from it. Still, she had to admit that she had never believed in higher consequences so she lived her life as if she could do anything and it didn't matter as long as she was enjoying herself. Self-gratification was what it was all about. Besides, didn't it make her feel good to have that kind of power? The power to make a man so weak with desire that he would forget that he had a wife and kids. The power to take everything from someone who had mistreated her so she could have the final word.

Never before had she looked at her life the way she had back there in that booth and now again in her room. These were always just things she had done. She had been young and living for the moment. She never felt bad about them until now. Tonight put a spotlight on something that had always been hidden in the dark and revealed just how truly repulsive it was. Something that should never be seen by anyone. The guilt and shame that had consumed her in that moment was surprising and frightening. Now it made her think, why had it never bothered her before? Her past had not changed. She had not changed. Somehow watching it from the outside gave her a perspective that she couldn't bury in the cat box. She realized that when she had looked on her past with regret, it was always for poor choices that had made *her* life worse. Never before had she acknowledged the things she had done to others in the past that had made *their* lives worse. She was faced with the horrifying truth that she wasn't always the victim. In some cases, she was the villain. She could have gone through her entire life without being confronted with this truth.

****

"I doubt we will see her tomorrow, Caroline." Jack looked at her skeptically.

"You will." She licked the sticky syrup from her fingertips. "And the next and the next and the next."

Taylor was studying Caroline closely. She was fascinating to be near and at first he had thought it was a dynamic personality that drew him in. It was apparent to him now that it was much more than that. He was convinced that she was not human. Just the thought of that made him feel like his cheese was sliding off his cracker.

"No." She looked at him sternly.

"I didn't say anything." Taylor leaned away from her.

"God already told you that you aren't crazy." She wagged her finger at him like a mother gently admonishing a child. "You aren't supposed to worry about that anymore, remember?"

"That's true." He sighed. "But how do *you* know that?"

"I was there." She said, staring into his eyes.

"At the church?" Taylor was shocked.

"Nope. I was with God." Caroline said and finished the last of her pancakes. "You going to eat that?" She pointed her fork at Jack's plate where his uneaten half Belgian waffle sat beckoning her.

"Be my guest." Jack said and handed the plate to her. He wasn't sure what to think about what she was telling Taylor. Logic told him she was a lunatic. His gut told him she was telling the truth.

"How is that possible?" Taylor had to ask but remained open minded. The calm that settled over him was comforting. He was in uncharted territory but it felt perfectly natural somehow. He had to face the facts that the Caroline situation wasn't any stranger than having God talk to him over the mega television screens at church.

"You know." She giggled and gave Taylor a knowing look.

"You're an angel." Jack said.

"Ding, ding, ding! And what do we have for him, Johnny?" She announced in a game show host voice.

"That explains a lot." Jack looked at Taylor. "You already knew, didn't you?"

"I suspected it before but I was convinced when she just appeared in the car back there." Taylor shrugged.

"Then you can answer a lot of questions, right?" Jack gave her an expectant look.

"Can and will are not the same thing." She pointed out.

"Understood." Jack nodded. "Will you tell me what happened to me in that park?"

"Yes." She answered happily. "But not tonight." She stretched and yawned. "Time for a girl to get her beauty rest."

"I suppose we need to get you a room." Jack offered.

"You're so cute!" She reached over and pinched his cheek. "That was my way of saying good night. I don't sleep. But you do and you two need rest. There is a lot to do tomorrow and our Kate is struggling with a lot right now. I need to peep in on her."

"Be careful." Taylor looked at her sternly. "It seemed like she'd just as soon stomp you into a puddle as look at you when she left."

Caroline leaned over and kissed Taylor's cheek. There was a tingle like pins and needles. "Don't worry, Papa Bear." Taylor slid out of the booth and let Caroline out. She turned and blew Jack a kiss. He rolled his eyes which made her giggle, then she literally skipped out of the Pancake House and disappeared into the night. When she was gone, Taylor sat back down.

Jack was grinning at him. "Just when you think things can't get any weirder… things get weirder." He laughed.

"Words to live by, my friend." Taylor chuckled.

They split the check down the middle and drove back to the hotel. Taylor was in his bed with the lamp on when Jack finished brushing his teeth and climbed   into the other bed.

"Do you think Kate is part of this?" Jack plumped up his pillows.

Taylor was lying on his back looking at the ceiling. "After what Caroline said, yes."

"I was afraid you were going to say that." He sighed. "You think she will help us find Rose?"

"Maybe. I feel like she is part of this, but I don't exactly know how or why." He turned on his side and looked at Jack. "Does that make sense?"

"Yes." Jack nodded. "But she is very… hmmm, what's the word I want to use? Unpleasant." He frowned.

"That's not the word you *want* to use, but I get what you mean." Taylor laughed. "I think she is just guarded, Jack. Perhaps if she feels like she can trust us, she will become more pleasant."

"Good luck convincing her to stay with us." Jack narrowed his eyes. "I can just see how that will go down. 'So, Kate, we're on a mission from God and we want you to join us to accomplish His work. You game?' I would duck when I say it if I were you because she'll start throwing things when she hears the name God come out of your mouth."

"Maybe we don't have to *do* anything." Taylor confided. "What if *she* comes to us?"

Jack laughed. "Your eyes are open, but you are dreaming, brother."

Taylor turned out the lamp and sighed. "Maybe. But a boy can dream, can't he?"

"Good night, old man." Jack chuckled.

"Night, kid." Taylor replied warmly.

CHAPTER 4

Kate got ready for bed but could not stop thinking about what had happened. It made her wonder if her life would have been better if she had the moral compass people claimed to possess when they got religion. The very thought of it made her sick. She had always regarded churchy people as hypocrites. They showed one thing to the world but lived their lives however they wanted. At least the people she had come in contact with over the years were that way. She couldn't recall having met a church person who wasn't faking it. But then again, how many church people had she actually met in her life? A handful maybe? Was it fair to judge millions of people based on a few? Good grief! Why was she even thinking about this? Had that little witch planted some kind of never ending conflict loop in her mind as well? Why would Caroline care about her life anyway? She didn't mean anything to these people. She had briefly crossed paths with them and it was clearly a one-time thing. 'See you tomorrow!' Caroline's voice rang in her head. "Not bloody likely." Kate said aloud. She got into bed and hoped sleep would come quickly. It did, but with it came dreams.

She was walking towards a beach where dark blue water lay just beyond the rocks and sand. The land around was hilly and trees dotted the landscape here and there. She noticed a man sitting on the ground in the shade of a tree. He wore all white clothing which was lightweight and moved easily with the breeze. His skin was tan against the white tunic style shirt. He had a beard and head of rich brown hair that the sun had lightened on top. It was long and touched his shoulders. She couldn't see much more of his face from her vantage point but she could see that his head was down and his eyes closed. His lips moved ever so slightly. Perhaps he was speaking softly to someone on the other side of the tree and she simply couldn't see them. Or he may have been singing for all she knew. He seemed very serene and she didn't want to disturb him but she began walking towards him anyway as if pulled by an invisible thread. As she approached he spoke, his head still down and eyes still closed.

"Katherine." He said. The sound of his voice stopped her in her tracks. Then he looked up with the softest, kindest brown eyes and his gaze fell upon her. The faintest smile graced his lips. His face was not what you would call conventionally handsome or extraordinary by most standards but it was the most beautiful face her eyes had ever beheld. She never wanted to look away. Ever.

Her eyes opened and she was wide awake. She moaned and turned over, punching the pillow next to her. "Why am I starting to have dreams at this point in my life?" She groaned aloud when she read the clock. 2:12 a.m. She lay there and thought about the dream, still very clear in her mind. There was something similar about this one and the one before. Part of it was how she felt. In these dreams, she felt different in her skin than she did in her real life. Also, the world felt simpler, smaller, and more peaceful. Was this man the man who everyone had been fussing about in the first dream? Somehow, she knew that he was. There was something extraordinary about him, wasn't there? It was an aura of contentment that surrounded him. It was remarkable. He seemed to be a walking, talking embodiment of all things good – like joy personified. Who wouldn't want to be as close to that as possible?

"Would *you* want to be?" It was Caroline. She was sitting on the edge of the bed looking at Kate. The love that shone in her eyes felt like a blow to Kate's gut. How could Caroline stand to be

194

near her, much less look at her with affection after knowing what she had done in her past?

Kate swallowed hard. "I don't know. Maybe." She whispered. Caroline reached up and wiped the tears from Kate's cheeks. Her touch made Kate's skin tingle. She started to ask how she got into her room then decided it wasn't important. She doubted Caroline needed to come in through an unlocked door like other people anyway.

"Can I ask for a favor?" Her eyes drilled into Kate's as if pleading. "Would you give the boys at least one week of your life? Just to observe." Then she grinned. "Think of it as research for a future novel." Kate would have said no, but that last part struck a chord. Sure, she could give a week in the name of research. That wouldn't be endorsing any kind of belief, right? She had plenty of time and she had no car so hanging out might work out okay. These men were making lofty claims. Perhaps it was worth a look see, for literary purposes of course.

"Strictly as an observer." Kate said reluctantly. "And they will be okay with that?"

"They will welcome it, Kate." Caroline assured her. "As for your other concerns, they don't know what you saw and I am not going to tell them. They are not judging you. I promise."

"I don't know what to think about what I saw. It was surprisingly awful." Kate admitted.

"You can't change the past, Kate. It's what you do with that knowledge going forward that counts." She patted Kate's hand and again the tingle set in.

"What do you mean?" Kate asked.

"We'll talk about that another time." Caroline said as she began to fade away and Kate couldn't see her anymore.

"I'm sorry I called you a witch." Kate said in a sleepy voice. She faintly heard Caroline giggle from somewhere very far away. She lay back down and was asleep again immediately.

CHAPTER 5

The next morning Jack and Taylor drove back to the Pancake House for breakfast. As expected, Caroline was already there digging into a massive breakfast of eggs, biscuits and gravy and French toast. She waved at them with her fork as they entered the restaurant. "Morning Glory!" She shouted to them from a small booth.

"You look chipper today." Taylor smiled at her as he slid in next to her.

"She's always chipper." Jack pointed out. "Good morning, Caroline."

"You boys ready for today?" She asked before taking a bite of biscuit dripping with white country gravy.

"Maybe." Jack answered. "What's supposed to happen today?" The waitress approached and put water and coffee cups on the table for the new arrivals and handed Jack a menu.

"Well, you never know now do you?" She smiled at him. "So, you should be ready for anything, right?"

"Good point, little lady." Taylor agreed as he took a menu from the waitress and thanked her.

They chatted about the food while they looked over the menu then gave Gloria their order when she returned.

"Alright Caroline. Since you have an inside scoop on everything, where are we supposed to go next?" Jack studied her. She was an eating machine, this girl. It was her super-fast metabolism she had said. That made him smile. Oh no. She was starting to grow on him.

"Can't tell you that." She gestured towards Taylor with her thumb. "This guy is getting all that information. I'm sure he'll agree that you're not going anywhere this morning, right?"

"I'm not feeling prompted to leave town just yet. Staying put for the time being feels right." Taylor agreed.

****

Kate rolled out of bed feeling energetic and refreshed. She watched the news briefly on TV. It was nothing but bad news – every day seemed to be worse than the day before. It was depressing to watch but she wanted to see what the weather was going to be like. She had to wade through the horror stories about racially motivated riots and looting in New York, and a two day old infant found in a dumpster in Kentucky barely clinging to life. There were more random terror attacks in Philadelphia, Seattle and Miami and tornadoes killed hundreds in Kansas, Oklahoma and Arkansas. Just when she didn't think she could take any more, they got around to the weather forecast. Hot and humid in this area of Missouri. She decided to shower and get dressed now that she knew what kind of weather to dress for. Shorts, tank top and sandals would fit the bill.

She sat for a while and thought about the previous night. It still weighed heavy on her mind and now that the seed was planted it was growing at an alarming rate. Guilt, shame, and regret were all swelling inside her. The dream about Caroline had been interesting to say the least. The thought of observing these self-proclaimed crusaders had its appeal and her brain was already buzzing with the plot for another story. It would be a departure from anything she had done before which was intriguing. But for all she knew they had already left town heading east to do whatever it is they do. If they had not left yet, it would not be too hard to find them. Horatio was a small town with only a few hotels. They weren't staying at her hotel so that only left a few other possibilities. She decided she would track them down and see if they would be willing to take her along for the sake of research. But that would have to wait until after breakfast because she was famished.

Kate walked across the parking lot to the Pancake House with visions of steak and eggs dancing in her head the entire way. She walked in and waited for the hostess. Before she could speak, Caroline pounced on her from the left and locked her in a bear hug. "Katie Bug!" She squealed. Once she got over the initial surprise of being blindsided, Kate noticed how freakishly strong the girl was. Caroline giggled and danced Kate around the foyer, still holding her tight with both arms. Kate was laughing in spite of herself.

The hostess was laughing with them. "Table for two?"

"No thanks, Lisa." Caroline released Kate and put her arm around her shoulder instead. "She's joining us back here." She gestured to a booth to their left. "Come on, Momma!"

"Thanks…" Kate was pulled away before she could finish thanking Lisa.

"Look who I found!" Caroline said to Taylor and Jack. They looked up and saw Kate standing there with Caroline practically draped over her.

"Good morning, gentlemen." She smiled at them and waited for Caroline to let her go. Finally, she did so she could get back to her breakfast.

"Good morning, Kate. You look lovely today." Taylor said genuinely happy to see her. Jack slid over to give Kate room to sit.

"Warmed it up for you and everything because I am just that awesome." Jack said, patting the seat next to him.

Kate rolled her eyes but she was smiling. "Thanks guys." She slid in next to Jack. Gloria came with water, coffee and a menu. Kate said she did not need to see the menu and ordered the steak and eggs. "I owe you all an apology." Kate said to them finally. Caroline was grinning, her eyes were wide and attentive as she chewed. "My rudeness last night was inexcusable and..." She was interrupted.

"Umm, you are using really big words." Jack said somberly. She looked at him unable to believe that he was implying he couldn't follow her vocabulary. He started laughing and then Taylor joined him.

"There is absolutely no need to apologize to us, Kate." Taylor said. "That's Jack's lame attempt at saying it's all good." She looked at Jack again and he flashed that movie star smile. She punched him in the arm.

"Fine. I really wasn't sorry anyway." She said and then laughed. She gave him a mean look from the corner of her eye. He was still laughing.

"Aw! See?" Caroline interjected. "We're all friends again!" She clapped her hands happily.

"I'm glad." Taylor looked at Kate. His eyes spoke volumes about sincerity. "I never want you to feel uncomfortable or unwelcome around us." He continued and she believed every word he said.

"I appreciate that. And I've had some time to think." She glanced at Caroline who winked at her. She knew exactly where this was going, didn't she? Maybe that dream wasn't a dream after all.

"Bingo!" Caroline mouthed the word to Kate. Kate's heart was racing. It was true then that Caroline was really something more than the rest of them were. Acceptance should be harder but for whatever reason, she found it easier today to accept the possibilities of the supernatural.

"I wanted to ask if you two would be open to letting me tag along and observe you in action for a week or so." She was ready for resistance or an argument and she had a lot more to say to sweeten the deal if they needed convincing. Turns out she didn't need to.

"Absolutely!" Taylor said, emphasizing it by slapping the table. "Jack and I were hoping you might like to join us." He was grinning at Jack and waggled his eyebrows up and down. Jack put his face in his hands and muttered something.

"I don't think Jack feels the same." She said. Jack raised his head and lowered his hands. His face was red and he had tears in his eyes. He was laughing. Hard.

"No ma'am." He said when he had the breath to speak. "I am definitely on board with you joining us for as long as you can stand us." He pointed his finger at Taylor and smiled. "I told you never, ever do that again."

Caroline's head snapped to her left and she looked at Taylor.

"You mean this?" He did it again. Kate and Jack both laughed and Caroline leaned back away from him.

"You could get a lot of women with that move." She said in a voice that expressed awe. That made Jack laugh hysterically. So, she knew about the conversation they had on the road when Taylor did it for the first time.

"But seriously." Jack said finally. "Kate, we are not exactly sure where we are going or what will happen, if anything. But we would love to have you come along regardless."

"Thanks for being cool about it, guys." She said, truly grateful that they were so accepting. "But I am warning you now, I'm probably going to have a million questions. Is that okay?"

"You bet." Taylor said. "If you will all excuse me for a moment, I need to visit the little boy's room." He stood up and headed towards the restrooms.

"I've never met anyone as nice as him." Kate said to Jack.

"Me either." Jack said. "He's one of a kind."

"And powerful." Caroline said to them.

"How do you mean?" Kate was very interested in hearing this.

"Unbridled faith and obedience are often rewarded with great power." She explained. "And he is following strict instructions from God Himself so even more gifts are given to him so he can complete his tasks."

"So, you believe that God spoke to Taylor and gave him a specific directive?" Kate wanted to clarify. "And that He bestowed powers upon Taylor so he could carry out this directive?"

"I don't believe that, no." Caroline looked deep into Kate's eyes. "I know it for a fact."

"And that is because?" Kate asked. *This should be good,* she thought.

"I was there when The Lord spoke to Taylor." Caroline said.

"You were with Taylor and heard God's voice?"

"He didn't speak out loud as you and I are doing." Caroline said. She held Kate's gaze and kept her mouth closed and Kate heard her speak inside her head. *"But for those with ears to hear, there are other ways to be heard."* Kate was clearly surprised and a little shaken.

"I see." Her hands were shaking when she picked up her coffee cup. She immediately put it back down. "So you were with Taylor and heard it too?" Kate made air quotes with her hands.

"I wasn't with Taylor." Caroline gave her an expectant look. She knew when Kate figured it out it would rock her to her foundations. She was getting ready to do damage control if necessary.

"Then you weren't *there* like you said at first?" Kate was confused.

"Kate." Caroline leaned in. "I was there" She pointed up, "not here." She opened her arms.

Kate struggled to process what she was saying. She was in heaven? That means she's an angel. If angels and heaven are real then that means God is real. And if there really is a God, then she has spent her life completely ignoring Him. She felt a panic attack coming. Jack reached over and put his hand on her arm. She immediately felt calm.

"It's true, she is an angel." Jack confirmed it. "She can appear and disappear without warning. When you met us, we hadn't seen her since Utah several days before. Then suddenly she was in our car last night." He grinned. "And she knows things no one could know. I'm not sure what else she can do but I suspect there is a lot."

"He's right Kate. So, I'm not a witch like you thought."
She poked her tongue out at Kate and laughed.

"I apologized for that." Kate said, ashamed.

"I remember." Caroline told her. "I've been called worse,
believe me. We're good, Toots."

Taylor returned from the restroom with a folded newspaper
in his hand. "Someone left this by the sink in the men's room." He
sat down and handed the newspaper across the table to Jack. He
took the paper and read aloud the classified ad that was circled.

212 East Street KC 3p 6/14. (Rose)

"You found this with the ad circled?" He asked Taylor,
rubbing the goosebumps that had popped up on his arms.

"Exactly like that." Taylor shook his head in wonder. "Just
sitting there by the sink. You know what this means."

"We're going to Kansas City." Jack said and leaned back.
"She'll be there, you think?"

"That's what it implies." Taylor said. "It's worth looking
into."

Caroline spoke up. "You need to bring Kate up to speed,
fellas. Since she's coming along she should know what's
happening."

Kate shrugged. "Your call, Taylor. You can tell me as
much or as little as you feel comfortable with." Taylor looked at
Caroline. He wondered how much to tell her. Should he give her
every single detail like he did with Jack? Or should he simply give
her the Cliff Notes?

Caroline's eyes blazed with excitement. She knew something. He wondered what was going on in the little head of hers. Finally, she reached over and patted his hand. Then she sat up very straight and said in a formal tone, "Full disclosure is in order, Sir." She saluted which made Jack laugh. She was so very odd.

"Since we cannot spend the entire day here in this booth, maybe we should finish breakfast then go somewhere and talk." Taylor suggested. "There is a lot to catch you up on, Kate. And if you change your mind about coming with us after you hear all of it, we will understand." Kate wondered what could be so bad that it would literally frighten her away. She had learned enough about them that if she were faint of heart she would have left by now. But if their story is that provocative, she wanted more than ever to explore it for her next book.

"I have all day." Kate said, opening her arms. "I'm all yours."

"Jack, you on board with all this?" Taylor asked.

"You know it, Pops." Jack winked.

"Aw!" Caroline cocked her head to the side and put her hands together to make a heart with her fingers and thumbs. "Pops."

Jack shook his head at her. "You're too easily moved. You know that?" Jack said to her.

"Maybe so. But I –." She stopped and looked at Taylor. "You okay, Papa Bear?"

"I feel so blessed." Taylor said. "I've lost a lot in my life but for all that was taken, I've received more back ten-fold. It has never been more obvious to me than it is right here, right now." Jack knew that he was referring to his son, at least in part. Replacing Brian was impossible. But he knew that Taylor saw him

205

as a son more and more every day they spent together. And he in turn had begun to see Taylor as a father. Calling him Pops just then had slipped out. He didn't even know how, because he never called his own father Pops. But it came out of his mouth as naturally as breathing. Clearly it had struck a chord with Taylor. Is that what Brian had called him, he wondered?

"Wait, is Taylor your dad?" Kate furrowed her brow. She thought she had heard Taylor introduce Jack as his buddy not his son.

Jack shook his head no. "We'll cover that today when we fill you in." He promised.

They finished breakfast and Taylor used his phone to locate a place where they could be comfortable and talk. There was a lake with a park nearby. He told Kate they would run back to their hotel for a bit and then swing by and pick her up in about an hour. Caroline left with Kate while Taylor and Jack found a store where they bought some folding chairs and a blanket they could spread out. Jack grabbed a small cooler, some soda, water, ice and fresh fruit. They loaded up the Maxima and went back to the hotel to change into shorts and tee shirts.

As they were driving back to get Kate, Jack asked, "Do you think Kate will run when she hears everything?"

"I really don't know." Taylor admitted. "I am sure the whole thing sounds crazy to anyone on the outside."

"I have to say, I was shocked that she showed up this morning." Jack chuckled. "But you knew. You said so last night."

"Remember, I don't take credit for anything I *know*. It's definitely not because I'm so smart I just know everything. Far from it. God simply assures me of certain things." He explained as they pulled up to the front of Kate's hotel.

CHAPTER 6

The dingy inner-city hotel room was stuffy and reeked of stale urine and mold. Sully, Berk, Finn and Taro sat around the small table waiting for Mary to arrive. The mood in the room was tense to say the least. They had been summoned for what they knew would be a most unpleasant scolding. Mary was not happy when she called the meeting.

Taro looked like death warmed over. He had a huge bruise on the side of his face and it was swollen to the size of a plum. An unlit cigarette hung from between his lips while he shuffled a deck of playing cards. It waggled up and down as he spoke. "What's the game, gentlemen?"

"Seven Card Stud." Finn piped up. He shrugged off the lightweight army jacket he was wearing and hung it on the back of his chair. His wiry red hair was unruly and he always looked like he had literally just rolled out of bed. He had a full but scruffy beard that was in serious need of a trim. His expression was neutral. No one had ever seen Finn happy or amused, probably because he was rarely anything but stoic.

Taro distributed the cards around the table while Berk dumped matchsticks and started dividing them up among the players. The game was about to begin when the door opened then slammed hard, making all of them jump. Everyone stood up and came to attention.

Mary walked into the room and it felt as if all the air was sucked out. In its place, there was an oppressiveness that hung like a thick curtain all around them. Her high heels clicked across the bare floor as she paced back and forth. She wore typical corporate business attire – a navy pencil skirt with a white blouse and matching navy blazer. Her long blonde hair was swept up in a bun.

"We have some things to discuss, don't we?" She said finally. Her full lips were tightly closed and only one corner of her mouth curved upward. All four of them nodded in response. "Sit down and pay attention." When she looked at Sully his mouth immediately went dry. "You were supposed to keep Jack from leaving Salt Lake City until Taylor was well out of range, correct?" She pulled a chair from the desk to her right and sat in front of them, crossing her legs, her foot bobbing up and down impatiently.

Sully cleared his throat and licked his lips. "Yes ma'am." He managed.

"Yet somehow he left Salt Lake City which means you failed." Mary glared at him. The others were barely breathing. They knew their inquisition was coming as well.

"Well yes, but it's not my fault." Sully's face was contorted with fear. His heart was pounding so loud in his ears he could hardly hear his own voice when he spoke. "He had protection and it threw everything off."

"Protection?" Mary narrowed her eyes at him. "Explain."

"Jordan. He showed up and ruined everything." Sully was almost in tears. He really had not wanted to mention Jordan to Mary.

Mary's jaw clenched and she sat in silence for a moment. So, Jordan was protecting Jack, huh? That certainly threw a wrench in the works. *But what's done is done*, she thought. *We move on from here*. At least now she knew who the players were. She hoped there would be no more surprises like this.

"That doesn't change the fact that you had a job to do and you failed to do it." Mary said flatly. She shifted her attention to Berk. "Once *he* failed to delay Jack in Salt Lake, you went into action to get him under wraps in Green River." Her green eyes

208

flashed at Berk. "And he got away. Are you blaming your failure on Jordan as well?"

"No ma'am." Berk said in a shaky voice. "I was able to get those kids to jump Jack and then they ended up tying him up in a building out in the sticks. I helped them set the place on fire with him inside. I thought it was all taken care of."

"You thought." Mary laughed. The sound lacked any humor. "Well, something went wrong because the very thing we were trying to stop from happening did indeed happen and Taylor found him." She got up from her chair and began pacing again. "Do I need to remind you yet again that Taylor was a threat all by himself? We suspected that he would be gaining reinforcements." She looked at them and sighed loudly. "There is strength in numbers. The whole plan here was to keep Taylor singled out and on his own. Alone he is more manageable, but now he has Jack and together they pose a greater threat." She studied the men in silence for a moment. "Taylor has been sent to find someone who is pivotal, gentlemen. We don't know who it is, but this person has the ability to tip the scales dramatically in their direction or ours. That means potentials for our side could be recruited for their side and as we all know once we lose them they are gone forever. I understand the number is astronomical so we cannot allow this person to be influenced by Taylor."

"Who is he? Or she?" Finn asked.

"No one knows." She frowned. "Not even Taylor knows but he is determined to find out. Right now, he's convinced he is looking for a female named Rose – why I couldn't say. There's nothing to support that this information is accurate but I can tell you he is more resourceful and powerful than you can imagine and he won't stop until he finds her."

"So, we stop him then." Taro said.

"Wrong." She swooped in and put her face right up in his and screamed "Wrong! Wrong! Wrong!" He squeezed his eyes shut and stiffened. Finally, she backed away. "It's exactly that pedestrian kind of thinking that has gotten us into the mess we're in right now. *We* also need to know who she is so *we* can recruit her for *our* cause. You guys just don't get it, do you? If it was that simple don't you think we would have just killed Taylor at the beginning of all this and called it a day? Hello? He is the only one who can find her. Period. No matter what we try we have no way of identifying this person. The only one with sight to see who she really is will be Taylor. We need him alive and searching until he does find her. But the more reinforcements he has around him the harder it will be to dispatch of him when the times comes." She waited for the lights to come on for these dolts. Finally, they seemed to be getting a clue.

"Okay. Yeah." Berk said nodding.

"Now can we get back to our meeting?" She shifted her attention to Finn. "You are the only one who didn't drop the ball. You were tasked with stealing Kate's car and you succeeded. However, we clearly underestimated the situation and she ended up on a collision course with Taylor and Jack anyway – something we wanted to avoid." She moved on to Taro and gave him a disgusted look. "So, we went to Plan B to derail Taylor and Jack so they were out of commission when she came into the vicinity. That's where you came in, Taro and all I can say is *epic fail!"* Taro stared at his hands, too ashamed to meet Mary's gaze.

"I got knocked out. That woman is some kind of Jujitsu expert or something." He stammered.

Mary threw her arms up in the air. "Really?" She looked at him, clearly astonished. "First of all, you should have heard her and/or seen her coming. You're an idiot, Taro. Utterly useless."

She tapped her foot on the floor, impatiently. "You wasted too much time trying to be dramatic and have dialogue and make it all about your big moment and you missed the window of opportunity. The result?" She walked to the table, placed both palms down, leaned in and screamed, "Now they are three strong, you morons!" She stood and clenched her teeth as she waited for calm to return to her again. They had to answer to her but at least they had her as the buffer between them and Cassian. She knew this was going to come crashing down on her head when it was all said and done. Cassian would want to know, why hadn't her people done their jobs and contained this mess? And these idiots thought they had it bad? She was infinitely more fair than Cassian.

"There's more." Berk finally spoke up. Mary let out a heavy sigh.

"Do tell." She couldn't wait to hear this one.

"I followed those kids that worked Jack over to a place where they partied. Taylor and Jack showed up there together but they were not alone." He couldn't meet her eyes.

"And?" She hissed at him, making a hurry up motion with her hand. Her patience was long gone.

"Caroline was with them." He said in a small voice.

Mary hoped she had heard him wrong. "What did you say?" She yelled at him.

He spoke in a louder voice this time, "Caroline was with Taylor and Jack."

Mary felt the last shred of self-control slip away. She made fists with both hands and her nails dug into the palms so deeply that blood began to stream onto the floor. Mary threw her head back and opened her mouth wide but her scream was inaudible. Suddenly the room became a vacuum, then the concussion wave hit and the windows, mirrors and television screen exploded all around them. The four men took cover under the table while blood pooled on the floor around her feet.

Once she regained her composure, Mary relaxed her fists and the deep wounds made by her long fingernails closed and healed immediately. She moved her head from side to side to stretch her neck muscles which had tensed up when she let loose on the room, then she took a deep breath. So Caroline was involved. Jordan was bad enough but Caroline was a game changer.

"Why did you tell her that?" Sully shoved Berk from where they were hunkered down under the table.

"Get up you morons." Mary said. "There will be no withholding information regardless of what the fallout may be, do you understand me?"

They climbed up from their hiding place and brushed shattered glass off the chairs before sitting back down. They all nodded that yes, they understood.

"Going forward when I give you a task to complete, you follow through to the end. You make sure everything I tell you to do is done and done completely. You got me?" She yelled at them. They were muttering and nodding in agreement, clearly terrified of her. "You'll be hearing from me. But make no mistakes, things are going to be a lot harder based on how far out of control this has gotten." She turned to leave and waved her hand in the direction of her chair which flew across the room and crashed into the wall behind them. The frightened men cried out. By the time they got themselves under control again they saw that she had left and the door was splintered and hanging cockeyed by a badly bent top hinge.

Sully pointed to the busted door and looked at Berk. "You're the one paying for that, you idiot."

CHAPTER 7

Caroline peeked out the window and saw the Maxima pull up in the hotel parking lot. "Your chariot awaits, madam." She said to Kate.

"You are very strange." Kate said to her.

"And?" Caroline grinned. "I'm growing on you. Admit it."

"Ugh. Whatever." Kate rolled her eyes and grabbed her bag. "You read minds, why do you need me to say anything at all?" They left the room and walked down the hall to the elevator.

"I'll meet you downstairs." Caroline said. Kate turned to reply but Caroline was already gone.

"Not impressed!" She called out as the elevator door opened.

She stepped inside and heard a far-away voice say "Yes you are!"

"Oh Geez, you're such a show off." Kate laughed. "I don't like you."

"Yes, you do!" Caroline said from beside her.

Kate jumped and stumbled back against the wall with her hand over her heart. "Seriously?" She shouted. "Are you trying to kill me?"

Caroline was giggling. "Of course not! I figured we could go ahead and dispel any possible doubts you may have that I am who I say I am. Consider it laying groundwork. You need to be open minded for what you are about to hear. And I assure you everything they tell you today is the truth."

"I will keep an open mind." Kate promised. "So, there is no need to do anything tricky again, okay?"

Caroline nodded yes as the elevator doors opened. They left the hotel and climbed into the back of the Maxima. It was a beautiful day in spite of the heat and humidity and the drive to the lake was quite scenic. They found a secluded area near the water on a gently sloping bank. The grass was thick and lush and there was ample shade from the large trees that filled the park. Kate and Caroline spread the blanket and situated the cooler while Jack and Taylor set up the folding chairs. Everyone except for Caroline took a chair. She opted for the blanket, lying on her tummy and propping herself up on her elbows. She lifted her bare feet in the air behind her. She looked like a kid about to hear a story and her eyes sparkled with anticipation.

"I think the best way to do this is for me to tell you some of my story and then Jack can tell you some of his and we'll take turns. That sound okay?" Jack and Kate both nodded yes.

Taylor recounted his story from the beginning and stopped at a certain point for Jack to tell his story from the beginning as well. Kate asked questions when things were not clear but mostly she tried to soak it all in. When Jack was telling her about the incident in the park and mentioned Jordan, Caroline squealed and shouted "Yay!"

Kate gave her a look. "Why are you so happy?" She asked.

"You'll find out later." She was sitting up now, crossed-legged.

Jack continued then Taylor took a turn speaking after a while and so it went until they reached the point where the two of them met. Jack got to that part first, telling her about what it was like to be tied up and knowing no one would find him out there and then suddenly he saw headlights. She had to admit, the story was fascinating. Then Taylor told about taking random back roads until he was "told" to turn in at the place where Jack was. Caroline had been right, if she was forming her opinion on the fact that everything had to be based on the laws that govern the world as she knew it, she would have found all this too fantastic to believe. But Caroline had already demonstrated that another realm was at work and in that realm all things were possible. It had prepared Kate's mind to accept what she was hearing. Finally, they got to the point in time where Kate had met and saved them.

Several hours passed as they talked. Throughout storytelling time, they dug into the ice chest and got drinks. Caroline attacked the chilled fruit. Kate joined her on the blanket at one point and snatched a grape out of Caroline's hand and popped it in her mouth. She bugged her eyes out at Caroline as she chewed, taunting her.

"You owe me a grape now." Caroline said matter-of-factly and without humor.

"Don't they teach you how to share in heaven?" She asked. Caroline responded by poking her tongue out. Kate laughed and turned her attention back to Jack and Taylor. "Okay guys, so this beautiful mystery woman, Rose is the object of this entire campaign, right?" Kate asked.

"In a manner of speaking." Taylor explained, "To find her is one thing. To make her a believer is an entirely different matter. There's no guarantee that it will be as simple as witnessing to her."

"Witnessing?" Kate was unfamiliar with the terminology.

"Sharing the gospel." Jack answered. "Telling her about Jesus – who He is and what He's done. Like I did with Hailey on the bus."

She nodded, understanding now. "Okay, I get that. But you

made that seem like a conversation Hailey initiated that just went in that direction."

"Sometimes that's how it works." Jack said. He stood up then joined her on the blanket. "Kate, I don't know what you think Christians are like but we don't walk up to strangers and just start telling them what to believe. I think you picture us as car salesmen who pounce on people as soon as they step foot on a car lot. You know, hard selling until the customers run away or buckle under the pressure and just give in."

Kate laughed. He didn't seem angry or offended. He seemed to understand. "That's pretty much exactly how I envisioned it."

He smiled warmly and patted her shoulder. "You aren't alone. A lot of people think that way. And there are some Christians who think that's a perfectly acceptable practice. But true believers know exactly how to witness without knowing that they know." He laughed. "That probably didn't make sense."

"It does. And I'm sorry for being so ignorant about it." She sighed and leaned back on her hands. "I had a couple of bad experiences where the caveman approach was taken with me. I ran away as fast as I could and I was more closed off to the idea than before."

Taylor spoke up. "Those kinds of people do more harm than they realize. Some of them are just so excited they don't know how to be subtle or patient. Some simply use poor judgement. But we cannot force someone to believe in God or love Him. All we can do is share what we know with those who do not yet know or believe and God takes care of the rest. God prepares the soil, adds the water, the sunshine and makes the seed grow. All we do is take the seed and poke it into the dirt." He leaned forward with a very somber look on his face. "But often the devil destroys the seed

217

before it has a chance to grow. He would rather the unbelievers never hear a single word about Jesus and His grace. It infuriates him when his hold on them is threatened. He will do whatever he can to stop that message from taking root should someone hear it."

"So, the devil is real too?" Kate sighed.

Caroline jumped to her feet and came around to sit facing Kate. "Oh, he is real all right! And it's not just him and his demons. You know, the evil ones you cannot see?" She told her. "He also has agents right here on earth working for him everywhere all the time. Some are willingly in his service and some are influenced or swayed. Some are tricked." She spun around and looked at Jack. "Now, to answer *your* question from last night. That guy from the park, Sully is an agent of Satan. And Billy, the boy who tied you up? He was influenced by an agent whose name is Berk. Taylor, you saw him there at the Mill that night, wearing a black hoodie with a red pentagram on it. Taro, the guy Kate knocked out last night is also an agent. Another one named Finn stole Kate's car."

Jack shouldn't have been surprised but he was, maybe just because his suspicions were finally confirmed. "And Jordan?"

Caroline giggled and clapped. "He's one of us!"

"One of you as in believers or one of you as in angels?" Kate asked.

"Jordan is an angel. He was protecting Jack." She said happily.

"An angel was sent to protect Jack?" Kate was impressed.

"Indeed." A man's voice said from behind her. She spun around and saw an exquisitely handsome young man with long blond hair and fair features. He was very tall and slender. Caroline was up and on the young man in an instant, hugging him and planting kisses on his cheeks. He laughed and scooped her up easily in one arm. He literally held her in the palm of his hand. Kate stood up and waited to be introduced.

"That's him." Jack said, standing up. "Jordan."

"I thought I would drop in." Jordan said with a dazzling smile. Kate's knees felt weak. He put Caroline down and walked over to Kate. He took her hand and kissed it softly. The same tingly feeling she got from Caroline only much stronger surged through her body. "Katherine. It is a pleasure." She felt faint. He caught her as she started to go down and eased her back down to the blanket then he motioned towards an empty chair and asked Taylor, "May I?"

Taylor was grinning from ear to ear. "By all means."

Caroline sat next to Kate and leaned against her. "I know, right?" She said nodding towards Jordan.

"I get why you are so excited when you hear his name." She whispered. She looked back at Jordan who winked at her. "Oh good grief." She said under her breath.

Jack went over to an empty chair and sat. "That's some mojo you have there, sir." He teased Jordan.

"They are both overreacting." Jordan said humbly. "It is good to see everyone together, safe and sound."

"So, you and Sully. There is bad blood between you two, isn't there?" It had been eating at Jack since the day of the altercation. "Is he immortal too?"

"No." Jordan shook his head. "Sully is nothing more than a person who has embraced evil and serves Satan. He will do anything he is told to do by his superiors. He has advantages over the average human but has no supernatural powers. He's a very bad man who is well connected, but ultimately nothing more than a minion. We have had our run-ins before, yes. I assure you he was not expecting to see me that day."

"And he backed down as soon as you showed up." Jack recalled.

"Yes, he knows exactly who I am and what I can do." Jordan smiled.

"And because you did show up, they know that Jack is special. Because he was protected by you." Taylor interjected.

"Correct." Jordan confirmed. "Their camp is buzzing over all this."

"They know Jack and Taylor have met then?" Kate asked.

"They were tracking all three of you since before any of you found each other." Jordan told her. "They did not want this to happen." Again, he held his arms out. "And that is another reason why I am here. To let you know that they are angry and dangerous."

"But if they are just humans there is only so much they can do." Kate said.

"Yes, if you are dealing only with the minions. But don't be so naïve to think that they won't start sending in the heavy-hitters when they see fit." He was looking at Taylor now. "You pose a huge threat to those in positions of power, Taylor. Because you are personally backed by God you are dangerous to them and their agenda."

"Their agenda being?" Taylor asked.

"Stopping you from turning a particular unbeliever into a believer." Jordan said then he and Caroline exchanged a look. He looked back at Taylor. "The balance of power lies within her,

Taylor. They want that power to shift to their side, not ours."

"Why is it that one person has heaven and hell playing a game of tug of war?" Kate asked.

Jordan looked into her eyes and she started feeling woozy again. "Well Katherine, imagine a very special girl inside whom lies a dormant gift." He paused and looked deeper into her eyes. She began to see a picture in her mind. It was a young faceless woman going about her life like any normal American woman. "And this gift is going to be awakened soon." Kate saw a small glow deep inside the center of the woman's body. "If it is awakened by a righteous believer like Taylor here, it will become an amazing and wonderful power that allows her to make believers of millions of people all over the world." She saw the glow become larger and brighter until it exploded a brilliant light from within the girl and erupted in pure joy to the ends of the earth. She saw it! It was spectacular! "But, Katherine. If this gift is awaked by Satan, there is a totally different outcome." She saw the same girl but what was inside her was black and festering and it began to grow, spreading through her body like a turbocharged cancer, devouring her and then reaching out beyond her body with tendrils of malignancy that destroyed everything it touched. It left everything in its wake writhing in agony, without joy, without love and without hope. The image terrified her. "Do you see why it is so important that Taylor finds her before the demons do?"

"But you said they were simply minions." Kate was suddenly very afraid.

"Ah, no. Remember I said that *Sully* is a minion. And the people that Caroline named are also minions. They are doing the grunt work. You see, they are the flunkeys but when the actual troops get called, the army Satan sends to fight will be made up of demons. Human lives will be lost. Make no mistake about that." Jordan warned.

221

"We will find her and we won't fail." Jack said looking at Taylor who sat quietly listening to everything.

"Katherine, there is real danger here." Jordan had moved from his chair and was now on his knees in front of her. "If you decide to move forward with us, you must do so with full knowledge of the possible outcome and you must be doing it of your own free will. Do you understand?"

Her mind was still reeling from the images Jordan had shown her. Scary yes, but also better material for her book than she could have hoped for. If these guys were about to launch into a full on battle for the sake of good to defeat evil and she could document it, then she was definitely in. "I understand." She told him. "I still want to tag along and observe. This is too good to pass up."

Jack looked at Taylor who smiled and nodded. Jack didn't understand how Taylor could remain so calm but he admired him greatly for it.

Jordan said goodbye to everyone then turned and started to leave. Jack followed and as soon as they were out of earshot of the others he said, "I'm curious about something. Caroline's reaction gave me the impression that you two are not equal in power."

Jordan nodded yes. "That is correct."

"Okay, because she was behaving like you are much higher on the food chain than she is." Jack chuckled.

"Oh no!" Jordan clapped his hand on Jack's shoulder. "I don't even come close to being able to do what Caroline can do. She is scary powerful, my friend."

Jack stood speechless as Jordan walked away and disappeared behind the tree line. He didn't expect to hear that at all. What they say about looks being deceiving was definitely true.

He was thinking *Imagine, that little tiny pixie Caroline* – And then she was next to him. "What about me?" She spoke and startled Jack enough to make him jump back a good foot and a half.

"You scared me half to death!" He was holding his chest.

"You people are so dramatic!" She giggled. "Pixies are cute, Jack. I don't mind being called a pixie. It's better than being called a witch any day." She spun around and skipped away.

Everyone helped clean up and pack up the Maxima then they drove back to Kate's hotel.

"May we pick you up this evening for dinner, Kate?" Jack asked before she got out.

"Sure." She said. "Give me your cell and I'll put my number in. You can call me when you are heading over." Jack handed his cell phone to her and she entered her number. She then called herself from his phone. "And now I have yours." She said and handed it back to him and got out. "Bye guys." She called out before they drove away. She entered the hotel and headed for the elevator. The moment the doors closed she was sliding down the wall and sitting on the floor sobbing with her hands over her face. She was overwhelmed to say the least. All the things she had heard and seen were bouncing frantically around in her brain. Everything they discussed was foreign to her. Her head throbbed and her emotions were in complete chaos. Had she really agreed to move forward with these people into possible danger for a book? Yes, she had. She wanted to blame it on the beautiful and intoxicating Jordan but she didn't honestly believe he had talked her into anything. It was her decision and she had decided to stay with them. *This book had better make me a billionaire*, she thought bitterly. *And in a hundred years, my work better be considered classic like Charles Dickens for crying out loud!*

Back at their hotel room, Jack excused himself to take a walk and come to terms with everything he heard earlier from Jordan and Caroline. Taylor stayed behind and used his quiet time to pray. He opened his eyes when he heard someone in the room clear their throat. It was Jordan.

"It has begun." He said with a sober expression that gave Taylor pause. "You are now complete."

"We are?" Taylor's voice sounded small and uncertain. "It has?" Suddenly he felt out of his depth. "Jordan, I…"

"Taylor, I won't lie to you. The stakes are much higher now." Jordan sat next to Taylor on the bed. "Because the three of you have come together, you are a greater threat than before. I fear you have underestimated the force that has been forged by your alliance. You alone were a great threat. You and Jack together fortified your strength. But with Kate…" He held up three fingers. "There is power here that I cannot even begin to explain to you. I know it and the enemy knows it. That means the gloves are going to come off and the other realm – the world beyond this one which you cannot see – will be spilling over into your reality. If you thought you had tapped into the supernatural before, you haven't seen anything yet." He put his hand on Taylor's shoulder. The man was trembling, but not from fear. Jordan knew it and so did Taylor. The trembling was anticipation and excitement.

Taylor smiled, his eyes blazing. "Let the thin veil between this world and the next fall away. We will find Rose and we will bring her to God even if we have to spill every drop of our blood to save her."

Jordan smiled and closed his eyes. "As the Father wills, let it be so."

TO BE CONTINUED

In Book 2

THE LAST ROSE-The Thin Veil

(Excerpt to follow)

CHAPTER 1

Once in her room, Kate collapsed on the bed and closed her eyes. She had walked away from the gathering at the park exhilarated, frightened and confused. Revelation upon revelation had left her with a million questions vying for her attention and demanding answers. But she had no answers. Finally, her questions ceased and sleep took over.

Soon she found herself in a busy marketplace where people milled about buying various types of food. Her stomach growled as she scanned the figs, pomegranates and grapes. She was thinking about what she wanted to eat when she glanced over and saw him sitting on a stone bench just outside the market, near a grove of trees. He was dressed in white, the same as when she saw him on the beach and he was smiling at her. She walked passed the fruit, forgetting all about being hungry and made her way to where he sat. She was a couple of yards away when a small child ran up to him. The little girl had a handful of rocks she wanted to show him. When she ran up, his gaze shifted to the girl and Kate noticed his expression was one of complete adoration.

"Teacher, Teacher! Look at these!" She opened her hands. He began inspecting the small stones. He spoke to her in such a kind manner. The love she saw in his eyes was indescribable. He spoke softly to her about each stone as he held them up one by one. It was as if she had brought him the most magnificent treasure in all the world and he was captivated by it. He pointed out the glittering colors in some stones and the lines and layers of color and texture in

others. He held up the last small stone, which was the perfect shape of a heart. He held it up to his lips, kissed it and handed it back to the little girl. Her eyes were wide with amazement. She dropped the rest of them and clutched the stone he had kissed against her chest. So much joy overcame that small face. Her eyes shimmered with tears as she sat at his feet and leaned against his legs. He placed his hand tenderly on her head and stroked her long, blonde hair.

"You are like this stone, unique in all the world." He spoke gently to the child. Then he looked up at Kate, his eyes piercing her very soul and said. "And you are my beloved." Kate crashed to her knees without warning. As her knees touched the dirt, her stomach took flight much like the feeling of taking a sharp descent on a roller coaster when your body fights gravity and you feel as if you may float off into space. The little girl looked up at him, still holding the heart shaped stone to her chest in her tiny hand.

Her small voice carried across the breeze as she spoke to him, "And you are mine." Kate felt her own lips moving to form the words at the exact same time as the girl spoke them. In that moment, she recognized the child. It was herself when she was 4 years old. She was even wearing the dress she had seen in a picture in her grandmother's photo album. The little girl reached for his hand and kissed it. Then she lay down and rested her cheek on his bare feet. She wrapped her hand around his ankle, still holding the small stone in the other hand and closed her eyes. She had a look of contentment unlike anything Kate had ever seen. Kate simultaneously experienced what her younger self was feeling. Not only the contentment, but

227

she could feel the softness of his skin against her cheek. How could that be? She was on her knees several feet away. As he reached down and touched the little girl's head, Kate felt the warmth of his hand on her own head.

He smiled and his face radiated infinite joy. "Will you come to me now?" He reached out his hands towards her. She reached both arms out for him and tried to stand but she couldn't move. No! Why couldn't she move? She wanted nothing more than to run to him but she was paralyzed there on her knees. Overcome by sorrow, Kate began to sob.

When she awoke in her bed, her pillow was soaked through with tears. Her cell phone began to ring. It was Jack. She answered, trying her best to sound normal.

"Are you okay?" Jack was concerned when he heard her voice.

"Yes. I'm sorry, I fell asleep. Just groggy. You on your way?" Kate wiped her wet cheeks with her fingertips.

"We're leaving now. We'll be there in 20 minutes if that's okay." He said.

"That's perfect. I'll be ready." Kate said. She hung up the phone and ran to the bathroom. She washed her face with cold water and stared at her red eyes in the mirror. *What had THAT been about?* She thought, recalling the dream. She had to sit down again and ended up on the edge of the tub. She was still reeling from the love and joy she had felt. But there was also sadness, wasn't there? That joy had been something she wanted but it was beyond her reach. Something she would give anything to have in her life, not just visit in a dream.

None of this made any sense at all. Three times she remembered having dreamed in her life and all three were about this same man in some foreign place. How odd was it that she would rather fall back into that dream world and live there? Well, why not? That's where he is and he is…everything. *Really Kate? A figment of your imagination is "everything"?* She thought, shaking her head free of the cobwebs. *You're an idiot. It was a dream. Get over yourself.* But she couldn't. If she knew how to find him right now she would scour the earth and never stop until he was within her reach. Even if she had only one moment in his presence, somehow she knew it would sustain her for a lifetime. Then her expression of hope changed to one of bitterness. "Too bad he's not real." She said to the face in the mirror. She turned out the light and went to her suitcase to change into a summer dress for going to dinner.

"Where's Tinkerbell?" Kate asked when she met Jack and Taylor in the lobby of her hotel.

"She took off again." Jack shrugged. "Of course, she could be here and we just can't see her." He looked around suspiciously. "You never know about that girl." Kate nodded, remembering the elevator episode.

"You look very fetching this evening, Kate." Taylor complimented her. "You make us look like bums."

"Hey! Speak for yourself!" Jack straightened the collar on his button-down shirt and pretended to lick his palms and smooth down his hair on the sides. "I'll have you know I put a lot of thought into this ensemble."

"You both look very dashing." Kate said sweetly and it was the truth. Jack was wearing jeans and a teal long sleeve button-down shirt with boots. His hair was gelled and perfect, as usual.

Taylor was clean-shaven and wore a black polo shirt with khakis and nice shoes. They both smelled wonderful. She was in good company. "Shall we go out and dazzle this little hamlet?" She hooked her arms in theirs. They left the lobby with all eyes on them, including a pair that was not welcomed.

www.ingramcontent.com/pod-product-compliance
Lightning Source LLC
Chambersburg PA
CBHW072353020726
47506CB00004B/1101